D0960585

HALF
IN LOVE
WITH
DEATH

Emily Ross

MeritPress | fw

Published by
Merit Press
an imprint of F+W Media, Inc.
10151 Carver Road, Suite 200
Blue Ash, OH 45242. U.S.A.
www.meritpressbooks.com

ISBN 10: 1-4405-8903-8
ISBN 13: 978-1-4405-8903-4
eISBN 10: 1-4405-8904-6
eISBN 13: 978-1-4405-8904-1

Printed in the United States of America.

10   9   8   7   6   5   4   3   2   1

This is a work of fiction. Names, characters, corporations, institutions, organizations, events, or locales in this novel are either the product of the author's imagination or, if real, used fictitiously. The resemblance of any character to actual persons (living or dead) is entirely coincidental.

Many of the designations used by manufacturers and sellers to distinguish their products are claimed as trademarks. Where those designations appear in this book and F+W Media, Inc. was aware of a trademark claim, the designations have been printed with initial capital letters.

Cover design by Frank Rivera.
Cover image © Shutterstock/Aleshyn_Andrei.

This book is available at quantity discounts for bulk purchases.
For information, please call 1-800-289-0963.

Dedication

For David, Thomas, and Julianne

Acknowledgments

Writing this novel was a long journey, but not a lonely one. Many people helped me along the way.

I am incredibly grateful to my agent, Rebecca Podos, for her steadfast belief in my novel, for understanding my story (sometimes better than I did), and for guiding me through revisions with her editorial wisdom. A huge thank you to my editor, Jacquelyn Mitchard, for her faith in my book and wonderful insights, to my copyeditor, Arin Murphy-Hiscock, for helping me to get my book through the home stretch, and to all the talented individuals at F+W Media/Merit Press for making this book a reality.

For starting me on this journey, thank you to my sister, Susanna Burns, who suggested I take a look at an old *LIFE* magazine article about the Pied Piper of Tucson, the case that became the inspiration for my book, and thanks for her continuing inspiration, encouragement, and creative ideas.

Enormous gratitude to my writing group—Kathleen Gibson, Elizabeth Esse Kahrs, Kate Leary, and Leslie Teel—for always providing the reassurance, and honest, insightful feedback I needed.

I feel very fortunate to be part of GrubStreet's community of writers, and am especially thankful for GrubStreet's Novel Incubator program. I am immensely grateful to my Novel Incubator instructors, or rather novel-whisperers, Lisa Borders and Michelle Hoover, for sharing their knowledge and passion for writing, and for believing in my novel with a faith that has sustained me on this journey. I am deeply grateful as well to the incubees (my Novel

Incubator classmates), Belle Brett, Amber Elias, Jack Ferris, Kelly Ford, Marc Foster, E.B. Moore, R.J. Taylor, Rob Wilstein, and Jennie Wood, for their encouragement and careful reads, and to all the Incubator alums for their ongoing support and friendship.

A warm thank you to the Massachusetts Cultural Council for the finalist award in fiction.

Juggling writing a novel with a full-time job and a family isn't easy, and I am grateful to my family for supporting my writing during this sometimes trying process. I'd like to thank my husband, Dave, for sharing my enthusiasm as I rambled on about my book, and for helping me make time for writing. Thank you to my son, Tom, for boosting my spirits with his exuberant and contagious love of the written word, and for assisting me with coming up with a pitch for my story. Special thanks to my daughter, Julianne, for reading an early draft, and for helping me polish my book right up to the end by giving me hours of her incredible editorial expertise.

My parents didn't live to see my book in print, but I am forever grateful to them for providing me with a home filled with a love of literature, teaching me to value creativity by the example of their own lives as artists, and for encouraging my writing.

CHAPTER 1

The night Jess left us, I sat on the front step twirling my little brother Dicky's top round and round. As I sent it spinning down the walkway and the black circles blurred into gray, I wanted to believe the stripes were really disappearing, that it was magic, but I knew it was an optical illusion. I was drawn to things that were not what they appeared to be. Sometimes I thought everything was an illusion.

I wiped the back of my neck, damp with sweat. It was getting late, but not a bit cooler. Darkness was erasing the green from the grass, the blue from the sky. The palm trees that lined our street looked like black cutouts. The swing sets were still. There were no more shouts of "olly olly oxen free." The younger kids who'd been playing hide-and-seek had all gone inside.

The time of day right after dinner sometimes made me lonely, but that August night I had something to look forward to. I was going to the drive-in with Jess and her boyfriend, Tony. My sister was seventeen, two years older than me, and she was in love with Tony. I couldn't wait for him to show up, take her hand and then mine as he turned to my dad and said, "I'll bring your two princesses home before midnight, Mr. Galvin. Promise." All the girls loved Tony, but he belonged to Jess, and when he took my hand I couldn't help but feel he also belonged to me.

I squinted at the distant place where the road met the desert, willing his gold car to appear. Behind me a door creaked open.

"Come in, Caroline. It's like an oven out there," Mom said. It *was* hot, but it had been hot ever since we'd moved to Tucson from Boston a year ago. I wanted to stay there and wait for Tony, but my thighs were already sticking to the step. I dragged myself up before I became a sweaty mess.

Mom and Dad sat in front of the TV with their scotches, Dad in his leather recliner, Mom on the sofa, smoothing her flowered dress. I stretched out next to Dicky, who was lying on the living room carpet, coloring. Spending summer nights with my parents bored me to death. I couldn't wait for my real night to begin.

We were going to the new Elvis movie, *Tickle Me*, and I was dying to see it. It didn't matter that Jess and Tony were only taking me to the drive-in because they had to. My parents actually believed I could prevent my sister and her boyfriend from making out. They didn't know that Tony was at least eighteen, and had dropped out of high school, and that I usually got out of the car to get candy and waited a while before coming back. Watching the movie from the snack bar was better than watching them kiss. I loved seeing the story unfold on the big white screen with cars in front of it, and the trees, moon, and stars behind it. It was magical when someone walked by and for a second became part of the picture. Sometimes I wished I could step out of my life and into a movie.

My parents didn't know any of this, and I'd never tell because everything that happened when I was with Jess and Tony was a secret. We even had secret names when we were with him; he called her Jezebel and me Twinkle Toes. Jess said if Tony gave you a secret name it meant he liked you. All I knew was that a glance from him could take my breath away.

I looked at my watch. Dicky bore down hard with his blue crayon. The ice clinked in Dad's glass. If Jess didn't hurry up, she was going to make us late for the movie. She made us late for everything. She didn't understand that events like sunset and darkness falling wouldn't wait for her to get her makeup right.

When she finally came downstairs her blonde hair was held back with a blue headband, and she wore pinstripe capris, a blouse knotted above her bellybutton, and white Keds. She stopped in the middle of the room and stared past us as if we weren't even there. Then she opened her big red purse and gazed into it as if contemplating the mysteries of the universe.

Dad looked up. "You're not going out like that."

Jess glanced around as though he couldn't possibly be talking to her.

Mom said, "Untie your shirt, hon."

"Geez." She undid the knot. "Happy now?" She glared at Dad.

I sat up. "Want to go outside and wait for Tony?"

She snapped her purse shut. "You're not coming."

"What? Why not?" I said.

She pushed her bracelets up and down her thin arm. "Something's come up."

Dad leaned forward. "What do you mean your sister can't go?"

She lowered her voice and said to Mom, "I can't take Caroline tonight. You have to trust me. I just can't."

"You always take her." Mom eyed her sternly. "What's going on?"

Jess craned her neck and glanced out the window, trying to see through space and time, right into Tony's blue eyes, wherever he was.

"I don't even want to go anymore," I said. Much as I hated the thought of being stuck at home, the last thing I needed was to be the reason Jess couldn't go out. I'd never hear the end of it.

"It doesn't matter what you want, Caroline," Dad said. "Jess is taking you, and if she doesn't, she's not going."

He gripped the arms of his recliner.

"You don't understand," Jess said. "I *have* to go." She set her lips in a firm line and looked through us with her cold green eyes. Then she headed for the front door.

Dad's face went from pink to red. I knew exactly what was going to happen next. I'd seen it a hundred times. Jess had a knack for pushing him and everyone else over the edge.

"Jack," Mom said.

He lunged past her. When he reached for Jess, she screamed, "Don't touch me," and shoved him away.

I held my breath.

Jess twisted the doorknob.

"If you step out that door," Dad said, "don't bother to come back."

"Mom," Jess pleaded, "I have to go."

"Just stay home with us," Mom said in the tearful voice she used when nothing else worked. Jess almost never listened to her or Dad, but that night, much to my amazement, she let go of the doorknob, ran her fingers up and down the gold chain on her purse, and pounded up the stairs.

When she reached the landing she gripped the wrought iron railing, narrowed her eyes at Dad and yelled, "I hate this place, and I hate you for making us move here." The bedroom door slammed. The color left his face. As usual, Jess had reached deep inside and found the worst possible thing to say.

We'd moved to Tucson because of Dad's great new job, but I knew the real reason was to give my sister a second chance after she'd gotten into so much trouble back east.

Dad started toward the stairs, muttering, "That ungrateful . . . ."

Mom put her hand on his shoulder. "Don't. She's not going to the movie. She's punished enough."

He settled into his recliner as if he were doing the world an enormous favor, and took a swallow of his drink. Mom spread the skirt of her dress out into a pale, flowered fan. A strained smile formed on her face. As she pushed a blonde curl behind her ear, the doorbell rang.

She stood, but Dad motioned for her to sit back down. "Let me handle this," he said.

I went over to the picture window that faced the street, and pulled aside the curtains. Tony's car was idling out front. In the hall Dad said, "Jess won't be going to the movies tonight."

"Can I talk to her?" Tony's voice had an edge to it.

"Jess won't be talking to you tonight."

I peered into the hall and saw Tony push through the door. He stood in front of Dad, a little too close.

"Hold on there, buddy. You stay outside," Dad said.

"I want to hear it from her, Mr. Galvin." He dug his hands into the pockets of his tight jeans. His blue shirt matched his eyes. I could see the polished, pointed toes of his Beatle boots with their thick Cuban heels. They were beautiful.

"What you want doesn't matter to me," Dad said.

"Don't have a bird, old man." He smiled at me as he backed slowly out the door and clicked it shut.

Dad reached for his drink. "That went well." He took a sip and set his glass down on the table so hard a wave of scotch splashed out. "I thought Arizona would be a fresh start for Jess, but she hasn't changed a bit."

Mom winced. "She didn't go out. She *is* better since we moved here."

He shook his head. "I hope you're right."

Some go-go dancers came on the TV. I liked watching them dancing in their fringed dresses and white boots, but Dad switched the channel to an old gangster movie. It figured. He absolutely loved movies, the older the better. After a few drinks, he'd go on about how he could have been a filmmaker if he hadn't had to get a real job as an accountant to support his family. Mom hung on his every word, because her lifelong dream had been to be a fashion designer for the stars. Jess wanted to be a movie star. That summer, everyone in my family wanted to be something other than what they were. I did, too. I just hadn't figured out what yet.

I turned back to the window. It was finally dark out. The coming attractions were probably already rising like giant ghosts from the desert, and I was stuck at home. Because of Jess.

CHAPTER 2

When I walked into our room, Jess was putting on makeup at her vanity. She turned to me, her mouth a shade of red called Cherry Madness. I switched on my bedside lamp with its pink, pleated shade that matched our pink bedspreads and flowered wallpaper. Mom had gotten a bit carried away with the color scheme.

As I opened up a *Beatles* magazine, Jess licked the tip of her finger, rubbed a spot of eyeliner off her lid and said, "Do I look like I've been crying?"

She did, but I wasn't about to tell her.

Outside of Mom, Jess was the vainest person I knew. People were always saying she and Mom looked like twins, and I was never included, even when I was standing right next to them. They were both thin, with blonde hair, pretty faces, and pointed chins, but their eyes weren't the same. Jess's eyes were green while Mom's were blue, but more than the color was different. While Mom had a way of looking at me that made me feel guilty for something I hadn't done yet, Jess's gaze went right through me as if I didn't even exist. It wasn't just me. Teachers took an instant dislike to her. She'd complain about the unfairness of this, and how she didn't understand. But I understood. Jess had the power to make people scream before she'd even opened her mouth, and it got her into a lot of trouble.

"Really, what do you think?" Her lips were pressed together in a superior smile. Blonde bangs swept in a curve across her forehead, and there was a whisper of blush on her smooth cheeks. Except for her red eyes, she was perfect, and she knew it.

"You look fine." I turned back to my magazine.

"Good," she said, "because I'm going out."

I drew myself up. "You're not going out. Dad said you couldn't."

"What he says doesn't matter. You'll figure that out soon enough."

"But he'll ground you for the rest of the summer if he finds out you went to the drive-in."

She frowned. "You need to understand. I have to go out tonight. Things are going on. Things I can't talk about." I nodded. Clearly something was going on because my sister hardly ever cried. Even when Dad completely lost it on her she would just yell back.

"Is this about Arnie?" She'd met Arnie a few weeks ago while we were on vacation in Los Angeles. When we got back, she and Tony had a huge fight about him.

She glared at me. "No."

I folded my arms across my chest. "You can't just say 'things are going on' if you aren't going to tell me more."

"I'm sorry, but I really can't tell you." She turned her gaze to the window, my moment of her attention gone.

I was fuming. I wasn't going to the drive-in because of her. She could at least tell me why. "Then I'm telling Dad you're sneaking out."

As I got up, she grabbed my *Beatles* magazine. "Don't you dare," I said, expecting her to tear it to pieces, but all she did was study it for a moment and then point to a girl in a photo. "Who's that?"

"That's Jane Asher, Paul's girlfriend." I loved Paul McCartney, with his angelic mouth and to-die-for eyes.

I waited for her to make some smart remark, but she just smiled. "You know you look a little like her, don't you?"

I gave her a skeptical glance. "Really?"

She turned my face toward her. "Your eyes slant down just like hers, and your smile is like hers, too. You look kind of British. If you curled your hair and cut your bangs, you'd look just like her. I'll help you with that tomorrow." She paused. "Is there someone special you'd like to impress? I mean other than Paul." She smirked.

My cheeks grew hot. She leaned forward. "Come on, you can tell me who."

I glanced away. "Billy O'Neil."

She laughed. "That freckled-faced jock who lives across the street?" I nodded. "Isn't he with Linda Beckham's little sister, May?"

I frowned. "Yeah."

"Linda is one super bitch and May is, too, but after I'm done with your hair, maybe you'll have a chance."

I smiled, wanting this to be true, though doubting it. Billy and I sometimes sat outside and talked about stuff, like whether UFOs were real and the meaning of life. But I couldn't get my hopes up. May was one of the prettiest girls in our freshman class. Her dad, Ron, was my dad's boss, and Mom thought we should be friends, but May barely acknowledged my existence.

Jess went on, "I need you to listen now. This is serious." For Jess, nothing was ever serious. "You have to promise not to tell Mom and Dad that I'm sneaking out. It's very important."

Her eyes opened wide, drinking me in. I paused, enjoying the fact that she actually wanted something from me. "Don't worry. I won't tell," I said.

"Good." She pointed to her red purse on the floor. "Can you hand me that?"

It weighed a ton. She'd probably stuffed a bottle of Dad's scotch in it.

She took it from me and opened the window, even though we weren't supposed to because the air conditioning was on. As she climbed out, she bumped her head, yelled, "Fuck," and punched the frame. She sucked on her fist.

I raised my eyebrows. "Hurry up or you'll miss the movie."

She gave me a blank look as if she didn't know what I was talking about. Beyond her, the night sky was sprinkled with faint, faraway stars. It was easy to grab onto the mesquite tree branch that almost scraped the glass and then drop onto the flat roof over the screened-in porch. From there it was just a short jump to the lawn. Jess had sneaked out this way before, and she never got caught. I figured Tony was waiting down below.

When she was halfway out she paused, sitting on the sill with one leg hanging out and the other in. Her green eyes rested on me for a moment. She started to say, "Would you . . ." but a car honked outside and she stopped mid-sentence.

"What?" I replied.

"Never mind." She swung her other leg over the sill. "Just remember, tell and I'll kill you," and then she was gone with a rustling, a thud, and the sound of a car peeling away.

"Mummy." A high-pitched voice startled me awake. My first thought was that it was Jess, but it sounded more like a scared little kid. Maybe my five-year-old brother Dicky had cried out in the middle of the night and I'd only dreamed it was my sister. I turned on my light. Her bed was still made up, the way she'd left it.

My heart was pounding so hard I thought it was going to explode as I walked across the carpet and looked out into the hall. I couldn't hear anything from Dicky's room. The bedroom doors were all shut. Everything was the way it was supposed to be.

I glanced at the alarm clock. It was just past midnight. Not that late, as far as Jess was concerned. With each passing second, what I'd heard became less real. It was probably just a nightmare. All I wanted to do was to go back to sleep, but my mouth was too dry. I drank all the water from the glass on my nightstand, but I was still thirsty. I wondered if it was possible to die of thirst in my own bedroom.

I went over to the window that I'd forgotten to shut, leaned my head out, and sucked in the hot air. Somewhere a cat howled, and I breathed a sigh of relief. That's what I'd heard. I glanced down at the street. Everything was the way it was during the day, only darker. Same old cars, same old houses, same old everything. Sometime before dawn, Tony would pull up in his gold car and Jess would step out quietly. She would slip in the back door and creep up the stairs with the stealth of a cat.

A desert breeze lifted the leaves of the mesquite tree. I thought of Jess sitting on the sill, half in our pink room, half out, beyond her the night sky, and beyond that everything else that was outside of our lives, like the world around the edges of the drive-in movie screen. She was out there now, having a good time, knowing things I couldn't possibly know. As I shut the window, I heard her say again, "Would you . . . ."

I wondered what she'd meant to ask me.

CHAPTER 3

Mom scooped some scrambled eggs onto my plate. My fingers trembled as I buttered my toast, careful not to crumble the bread with my knife.

Dad peered at me over his paper. "That lazy sister of yours still asleep?"

I took a long swallow of orange juice.

"Caroline?" He raised his eyes.

My heart was going a mile a minute. Jess hadn't come home last night. I wanted to just get it over with and tell them, but she'd be so mad at me if I didn't keep her secret. "She'll probably sleep until lunch." I opened up my *Beatles* magazine.

Mom leaned forward. "You know we don't read at the table."

I glanced up. "Dad is."

She folded her napkin. "That's different. That's the news."

Dad eyed me. "Look at this. Your favorite group is in the paper."

I took it from him and read, "August 15, 1965, will go down in history as the day the Beatles packed Shea Stadium with 55,000 screaming teenage fans." I frowned. While I was sitting alone in my room, history was being made. If we hadn't moved to Tucson, maybe I could have been there.

Dad shook his head. "Kids today don't want to work, don't want to be part of society. All they want to do is go crazy over the Beatles. Isn't that right, Caroline?" He elbowed me.

"God. Stop it, Dad," I said.

He sighed. "I wish I didn't have to work at a job I hate, but then we wouldn't have all of this." I winced as he gestured at the small kitchen.

Mom brushed some crumbs from Dicky's face. "I worry that this country is about to fall apart."

"You should be worried," Dad said. "Everyone should be."

I forced down another bite of eggs, and went back to my room. When I opened the door, I felt a sting of disappointment. I'd hoped that Jess had slipped in unnoticed, but she hadn't. My parents acted like they understood everything that was wrong with the world, but Jess was probably with Tony right now, hungover, and they didn't have a clue.

I sat down at my desk, piled high with books from the summer reading list for the AP English class I was taking in the fall. Even though I only had to read three from the list, Dad had bought me every single one. Everywhere we went he would introduce me by saying, "This is Caroline, top of her class." And then he would turn and say, "And this is Jess."

After she got suspended for drinking in school back east, my parents sent her to a fancy performing arts school in Boston they thought would be perfect for her. It made me ill. I was the one who did well in school, and I had to go to public school. Jess lasted three months before she got kicked out for stealing booze with some boy.

I pulled *The Doors of Perception* from my pile of books. It was really short and about drugs, so I figured why not. My teacher was pretty cool to have put it on the list. If Jess were here right now, she'd probably be saying something like, "Caroline, if you want to learn about drugs you don't read about them. You take them." I looked around at our pink walls, the pink bedspreads, our pink princess phone. Dust motes danced in the sunlight.

Her clothes were strewn all over the place, black lace bra and jeans on the back of a chair, one of her favorite white shoes on the floor. I loved those shoes. They had a white rose on the toe and a low heel. I slipped it on and limped around looking for the other one, but I couldn't find it. It was probably buried under all her other beautiful shoes in the closet.

As I took it off, I remembered the voice I'd heard in the night. Mummy was what Jess had called Mom when we were little. I'd called Mom that sometimes, too. I bit my nail. Everyone had bad dreams. Jess was going to waltz in whenever she pleased, without having given any of us a second thought. I'd be a fool to let her ruin my day.

I put on my op art bathing suit with the swirling black-and-white polka dots that went perfectly with the daisy necklace I'd made from black-and-white seed beads, grabbed the book and my *Beatles* magazine, and went outside to lie by the pool.

After rubbing on some suntan oil, I stretched out on a chaise longue. The turquoise water was flat and still. A couple of leaves from the orange tree that grew on the patio rested on the surface, not moving. Before we came here, Mom had raved about the beauty and wonder of that tree, but the oranges turned out to be dry and bitter. I reached down and grabbed one that had fallen next to my chair, flung it into the pool and opened *The Doors of Perception*.

This quote at the beginning knocked me out: "If the doors of perception were cleansed every thing would appear to man as it is, Infinite."

I'd always suspected that. When I was younger I used to do magic tricks, but to be honest, I stunk at them and they bored me. Now what interested me was real magic. I was convinced there was a whole other world out there where strange and impossible things could actually happen. It was just a matter of finding it.

Mom walked onto the patio with Dicky. "We're going shopping to buy some fabric, want to come?" she said.

I shook my head. The last thing I wanted to do was to go shopping with her.

She went on, "That's too bad. I'm making new living room curtains, something to brighten things up. What do you think of lemon yellow?"

"Lemon yellow sounds fine." Her cheerfulness annoyed me. I'd made hardly any friends here, and we were practically living *in* the desert. Did she actually think new curtains would make any difference in our lives?

She took a deep breath. "Jess sure is sleeping a long time. Give her a nudge. It's not good for her to sleep the day away."

A cold feeling passed through me. It had to be at least noon. Where was she? If she wasn't home by the time Mom got back, I'd have to say something. I heard Mom's station wagon pull out of the driveway. Dad was playing golf, as he did every Saturday. I switched to my *Beatles* magazine and studied Jane Asher's photo, her flowered mini-dress, her long bangs, her soft smile, her downward-slanting eyes that were like mine, her nose that was a little too big. I was thinking maybe I really did look like her, when something rustled on the other side of the fence. My hand tightened on my magazine.

I thought Jess might be sneaking in through our neighbor Debbie Frank's backyard, but when I peered over the fence, Debbie was walking toward me. This was strange. She hung out with Jess and Tony sometimes, but she almost never talked to me.

Her white-lipsticked mouth parted in a grin. "Hi, squirt," she said. She wore a sleeveless dress with a red patent leather belt. Her dark hair was teased up on top, with a spit curl pressed against one cheek.

Jess called Debbie trashy. Mom did, too, but she was polite at least, while Jess was downright mean to her. Jess said Debbie was as cold as a robot, and dumber than one. Mom said you should never taunt someone for being less than you. You should feel sorry for them, but never let on that you feel sorry. I wasn't sure Debbie needed anyone to feel sorry for her. There were rumors she'd beaten a girl up just for looking at her the wrong way.

"What have you got there?" She eyed my magazine.

I blushed, embarrassed to be holding it. "Something about the Beatles."

"Let me have a look." As she glanced through it, cigarette dangling from her mouth, I tried to summon the courage to ask if she'd seen Jess.

Before Jess dated Tony, Debbie had dated him, though Jess said that Tony just used Debbie. When I asked what she meant by that, she laughed and said, "Boys like Tony have needs, and girls like Debbie are easy." I stared at Debbie now, looking for signs of easiness. Was it her dull eyes with black eyeliner extending like wings from the corners, the way the top few buttons of her dress were undone, the way she didn't bother to push up her bra strap when it slipped below her sleeve?

"Cool." She handed the magazine back to me. "You got a favorite Beatle?"

"Paul," I said.

"Yeah, he's the sweet one. I like John. He's got a little meanness in him. I like my guys with a bit of meanness."

"I wish I could meet Paul."

"Hold tight to those dreams." She touched the small red velvet bow in her hair, and glanced back at her yard like she was thinking of leaving.

I struggled to clear my throat. "Have you seen Jess today?"

Her eyes widened. "No."

"She didn't come home last night," I said.

She leaned closer and whispered loudly, "That's not surprising, considering she's on her way to California. Your sister sure is something, just taking off last night like that."

"California?" I felt faint. Through a fog I heard her saying something like, "Didntchuknow?" I backed up, unable to feel my feet.

"Caroline, wait up," she said. "I can't believe Jess didn't tell you she was running away. I thought you'd be the first person she'd tell other than Tony."

I stopped backing up. My heart was beating so hard I worried I was going to have a brain aneurysm and drop dead on the spot like one of my uncles had. "Did Tony go with her?"

"No, and he's pissed." She folded her arms across her chest. "She's going to see some guy named Arnie."

"Is he driving her?"

Debbie shook her head. "I don't think so."

"Then who is?"

She shrugged. "Beats me."

I stood there, letting the possibility that Jess was miles away sink in. This was why she'd insisted that I not tell anyone about her sneaking out. She needed time, lots of it, so she could get away from all of us.

"I doubt she'll get very far," I finally said. "She's probably on her way home right now."

"Sure she is," Debbie said with a funny half smile. I stood there, unable to move, as she went on, "Gotta go, 'cause I'm going out with Tony tonight." She eyed me just to make sure I'd heard that last part and then left, her hips swaying as she walked across the green lawn through sun and shadow. I watched as she gave me one last backward glance. She didn't wave or anything. All she did was stare. Trash, I thought.

I went up to my room to figure out what to do. I had to tell Mom that Jess was on her way to California, but if I told her she'd know I'd lied, and I never lied. Maybe Jess would get bored like she always did, and make the guy turn around and drive her home. She could still walk in at any minute. Or maybe she really was going to see Arnie, or couldn't wait to start her movie career.

When we went to California to visit my aunt Lila, my parents shamelessly encouraged Jess's Hollywood dreams, probably because they hadn't realized their own. They made sure she saw everything—Madam Tussauds wax museum, Sunset Boulevard, Grauman's Chinese Theatre, and Schwab's Pharmacy where Lana Turner supposedly was discovered. Jess was obsessed with Lana Turner. She was under the delusion that they looked alike. Beverly Hills was my favorite. I loved the mansions with red-purple bougainvillea dripping over their high white walls, and the hint of movie stars in the air.

I pulled out the blue glass stopper from the bottle of Shalimar on her bureau and sniffed. It had a thick, sweet smell, like velvet flowers. I repeated to myself, "She's on her way to California."

CHAPTER 4

Slanting sunlight made every detail in the kitchen stand out—the ceramic rooster hanging on the wall with its creamy wings and blood-red comb, the shiny teapot on the stove, the wallpaper printed with clocks with vines slithering around them. Mom and Dicky were back from shopping and he was having an early dinner.

She pointed toward a bolt of yellow cloth on the counter and asked if I liked it. As I nodded, I had the weird sensation that something big and wide was watching through my eyes. It wasn't me, but was me at the same time. God? It didn't feel like God. It was more as if I was spying on this world that I used to be part of, but was part of no longer.

Mom smiled. "Jess will be happy to know we're having her favorite, tuna casserole."

Without meeting her gaze I said, "She's not home."

"She sure doesn't like to spend much time with us," she said.

Dicky plucked a pea from his plate. "I saw her hiding in the tree last night."

Nervousness crept through me, like wind rippling water. He must have seen her climb out the window. I turned to him slowly. "No, you didn't."

"What's he talking about?" Mom fiddled with her gold watch.

I shrugged. "You know how Dicky makes stuff up." It felt like the room was getting smaller and smaller. Soon the walls would close in on me.

Mom's expression softened. "Would you like an early dinner, too?" Before I could answer, she went on, "You don't have to wait. Dad's always late from golf, and Jess, well you know how she is. I wouldn't wait for your dad if I didn't have to. I get so hungry, but he'd have a fit if I ate before him. He does like his little rituals, and supper is one of them." Her words were like pebbles pelting me. I couldn't take it any longer.

"Mom," I said.

"What?" Her oblivious look made me feel sick.

"Jess isn't coming home. She's on her way to California." An inappropriate smile crept across my face the way it did when I was nervous.

Mom dropped the serving spoon she was holding. "Is this a joke, because if it is . . . ."

"I'm not joking. Debbie Frank told me."

"Debbie Frank. Why were you talking to her?"

"She came over when I was out by the pool. She said Jess is going to see Arnie."

"Arnie?"

"You know, the boy she met while we were on vacation." I felt less alarmed as I spoke. Jess was having a second vacation while I was stuck here. It was so typical.

Mom shook her head. "This doesn't make any sense. Jess slept late, and then she went out. She didn't go to California."

I got a sour metal taste at the back of my throat. "Jess didn't sleep late. She snuck out last night and didn't come home. She probably left for California hours ago."

For a moment Mom didn't move. "And you waited until now to tell me?" She was almost shrieking. "You lied to us?" Now she was definitely shrieking.

I wanted to shrink down to nothing. "She told me not to tell."

A spider with delicate, horrible legs ascended a thread dangling from the kitchen light.

"Caroline, you know that by waiting all this time to tell me, you may have put your sister in danger."

"I was afraid she'd be mad if I didn't cover for her." I struggled to avoid her guilt-inducing eyes as I went on, "I thought she was going to do the same stupid thing she always does, that she would stay out late and then lie to you about it, and you would believe her like you always do. I didn't know she was going to California."

"Is Tony driving her?" Mom's voice trembled.

"No, some other guy. Debbie didn't know him."

"Oh God, Jess is driving across the desert with some stranger."

I tugged on a hangnail with my teeth. The idea of Jess being in the desert hadn't occurred to me. Mom crumpled Dicky's napkin while he watched, his eyes wide. "She can't have gotten very far. We have to find her before it's too late. I'm going to call Debbie right now. Hand me the phone." When I didn't immediately jump, she said, "Now!"

She held the receiver to her ear for what felt like forever. "Why can't those damn people answer? What's wrong with them?" She jammed it back into its place on the wall. "Where the hell is your dad? He should be done with golf by now. He's probably at a bar, getting soused while Jess is God knows where."

Dicky yelled, "There's a mushroom in my mouth." He spit it out into his napkin and started crying. He'd hated mushrooms ever since Dad had told him about the poisonous ones.

He was working himself into a frenzy when Mom said, "Stop it," and for once Dicky actually stopped. The room fell silent.

Mom stared at the phone. "What are we going to do?"

We? I couldn't believe she'd said that. She was the mom. She was supposed to have the answers. I patted her on the shoulder and said,

"Don't worry, she'll come home soon. I bet she'll walk in the door any minute."

She didn't seem to have heard me. "I should call the police, but I hate to do that without your dad here." She turned to me. "Do you think I should call them?"

I took a deep breath. "Yes, I think you should call them."

Dad came home about fifteen minutes later, and a policeman showed up right after him. While they all talked in the kitchen, I sat in the living room with Dicky, chewing on my hangnail until it bled. I overheard Dad saying something about Jess being with Tony. Then Mom began crying and saying what a good girl Jess was. I worried that she'd tell them I'd lied about Jess. If the police found out they might arrest me. One of Jess's friends got arrested just for talking back to her mother. I looked out the window, still hoping to see Jess come walking up through the blue shadows, but the street was dark and quiet.

"Caroline," Mom called out. "Please come in here." My heart almost stopped.

She pulled out a chair and I sat down. "Officer Barnes wants to talk to you."

The policeman stared at me from the opposite side of the kitchen table. His light blue eyes reminded me of those husky dogs that live in the Arctic. I sucked on my hangnail, cold and sick at the thought of how much trouble I could be in for not telling on my sister.

"Your mother already told me what Debbie said, but I'd like to hear it from you," he said.

Dad frowned. "Just tell the truth." I hated the way he said that. Mom must have already told him everything. There was a tickle-feather feeling in my throat. I opened my mouth but no words came out.

Mom handed me a glass of water, her polished pink nails curved around it. I gulped some down, and in a voice barely above a whisper I told him how Debbie had said that Jess had gone to California with some stranger, and that she was going to see a boy named Arnie. I explained that she'd met Arnie in a souvenir shop in Venice Beach, and they'd gone out a few times, but I didn't even know his last name.

As I spoke, Officer Barnes smiled and jotted things down in a little notebook. He didn't seem as scary anymore, just a guy with strange eyes who really wanted to listen to me, maybe more than anyone else ever had.

When I was done he turned to Mom. "Mrs. Galvin, do you know how to get in touch with Arnie?"

"When we were visiting my sister, there was a sweet boy Jess liked, but I didn't catch his name." She glanced helplessly at Dad, unwilling to admit that they'd been too busy getting hammered by the pool with my aunt and uncle to notice anything.

Officer Barnes smiled. "She's probably at a friend's house, afraid you're mad at her for not coming home, but just in case, give your sister a call and let her know Jess might be on her way there, and see if she knows how to reach Arnie." He paused. "Lots of kids in Tucson are running away. Hardly a day goes by when we don't get a call from frantic parents. It's happening all over the country." My parents stared at him in shock as he went on, "It would be helpful if someone had heard her say anything about where she was going, or seen if she took a bag with her. For a trip to California, she would have packed some things."

He glanced my way. Any minute I thought I might forget how to breathe, as in the most casual voice, he added, "One other thing. Your mom said Jess snuck out last night but that you didn't tell her until dinnertime." I froze. This was it. My parents had given me up and now I was going to be arrested. "Is there a reason you didn't tell her?"

I looked from Mom to Dad. My pounding heart was all I could feel. Those pale blue eyes with the black dots for pupils were all I could see. My voice shook. "She said she would kill me if I told."

"Does she say things like that to you a lot?" He gazed at me sympathetically.

I smiled, nervous and relieved at the same time. This man who I didn't even know understood what a pain Jess was. "She does."

"Is there anything else you want to tell me?"

I nodded. "She had a fight with Dad because he wouldn't let her go to the drive-in. She fights with my parents all the time. She never does what they tell her. But last night was different. She was really upset. She said she had to go out, but she wouldn't tell me why." I wiped my sweaty hands on my thighs.

"Right before she left she started to ask me something, but then she stopped. Now maybe I'll never find out what it was." Tears crept into my throat. "I'm really sorry I lied about her, and I wish I knew more. All I know is she climbed out the window and she didn't take a bag with her. The only thing she took with her was a red pocketbook." I paused. "There might have been a bottle of Dad's liquor in it."

Mom looked at me in horror.

He patted my hand and thanked me for helping out. Then Mom gave him a photo of Jess and he said he'd cruise around the places where kids hung out to look for her. Dad said he'd drive around too and talk to Tony, but Officer Barnes asked him to wait until he'd had a chance to talk to Tony first.

"Don't want to spook the kid," he said with a funny smile.

Dad grumbled, "Okay."

When Office Barnes was gone, I watched Dad drive away down the street. What did he think he was going to find? He had no idea where Jess hung out. He should have asked me. I knew where she hung out, even though she hardly ever took me with her. I knew about the guesthouse behind Tony's parents' house where he lived on his own. And about the parties Tony and his friends had in this place in the desert they called "the drinking spot." I knew about Speedway Boulevard where kids cruised up and down in their cool cars. I'd seen it from out of Tony's rear window. I knew about the Hi-Ho Club where Tony took Jess sometimes. I'd never been in it but I'd imagined myself there, imagined the colored lights, the sparkling dresses, the love swirling all around. I knew about Johnie's, where we went sometimes to get burgers and shakes. And of course I knew about the Cactus Drive-In, where I hadn't gotten to go the night before. On any summer night half the kids in Tucson could be found at these places, and I was pretty sure Dad didn't know about any of them.

CHAPTER 5

While Dicky ran in and out of the sprinkler, I painted my toenails purple. Each tiny brushstroke left a violet jewel-drop. I needed something to be happy about, even if it was just my toes. It had been a week and Jess was still missing. Dad hadn't found her, and neither had the police. My parents were going to do a television interview to get the word out about her. I thought if Jess saw me on TV she might change her mind about running away, and begged them to let me come with them, but they said no. They were on their way to the studio now. As always, I was left behind.

Dicky's stuffed blue rabbit sat on the front step next to me, looking pathetic. Mr. Rabbit had been Jess's, mine, and then Dicky's. He dragged him around everywhere, holding him close and inhaling his sour smell, and he was always losing him. So far he'd left him at the playground, in a department store, and at the movies. Each time we would carefully retrace our steps, never quite believing it would work. But we always found him.

I stared down the empty street, wishing I could follow Jess's footsteps. If you kept walking, eventually there were fewer and fewer houses, the trees got smaller, and the grass stopped growing. Soon all you would see was sand and diminishing dots of green, all you would hear was wind whistling through dry grass. I hated the desert more than anything. It made me feel like I was at the end of the world; one more step and I would disappear.

I was stroking Mr. Rabbit's soft ears when Billy O'Neil came walking across the street, holding an orange soda. He offered me some and I took a long, cold swallow. It seemed like so long ago that I'd talked to Jess about him.

He sat down next to me, picked up the rabbit, and grinned. "Yours?"

I rolled my eyes. "Dicky's."

He glanced at the top hat and black silk scarf beside me. "Are you a magician?"

I brushed some dirt off my purple toenails. "Not really. Dicky wants me to make his rabbit disappear."

He stared into Mr. Rabbit's blue-button eyes. "Any more news about your sister?"

For a second I couldn't breathe. "My parents are doing a TV interview right now. I'm sure she'll come home soon."

He turned to me. He had red hair and so many freckles, it was like there was no space between them. "It must be hard not knowing where she is."

I inhaled deeply. Everything became so still and strange, it was like I was looking through a door of perception. The leaves of the mesquite tree were like brushstrokes. Dicky stood like a doll beneath the glittering droplets from the sprinkler. A ray of sun touched the metallic blue gazing ball in the middle of the yard.

"It's been hard for me, too, having my brother Steve in Vietnam," he went on. "Playing football won't be the same without him here."

I nodded. Billy's brother had been a star football player, and Billy probably would be one, too. Everyone was surprised when Steve joined up, but Officer Barnes was right. Lots of kids were leaving Tucson lately. A few, like Steve, went to war. Others, like Jess, ran away. And not all of them came back. I felt sick to my stomach as I went on, "We thought Jess was going to California to see this boy named Arnie, but my aunt Lila talked to him and he had no plans to meet her." I stared down at my hands. "Now we don't know why she's going to California."

Billy turned to me. "Maybe she isn't."

"Why would you say that?"

"'Cause it's logical."

"But her friends all say she's going there."

His knee touched mine. "Maybe her friends are lying."

"Why would they lie?" I glanced away. "I hate myself for not saying anything when I saw her sneak out."

"You can't always say something when you need to." He fixed his serious brown eyes on me and tears flowed down my cheeks, though this was the last thing I wanted to happen. This whole week I hadn't cried once. I felt embarrassed, but Billy just patted me on the shoulder with his freckled hand.

I wiped my eyes. "How's May?"

"We broke up." He tossed the rabbit in the air and caught it. "I can help you with the trick, if you want me to. Steve and I used to do magic all the time."

He put Mr. Rabbit in the hat and covered him with the black silk scarf. When he stepped away, it really looked like there was nothing in the hat, but then he pulled the rabbit out as if from nowhere.

We called Dicky over from the sprinkler. Each time we did the trick, he shrieked with glee. He finally got tired and went inside to watch TV. We paused at the gazing ball as I walked with Billy toward his house.

"How'd you do that without him seeing?" I said.

He smiled. "People never look too close. And not just little kids. Everyone wants to believe in magic."

"I want to believe in magic too, but not the silly trick kind. I want to do real magic." Billy cocked his head. I forced myself to go on. "Like knowing what people are thinking by slipping into their eyes or . . . ." I took a deep breath. "Passing through a wall and touching a ghost on the other side." I put my hand on the gazing ball and stared into its shiny blue depths, wishing I could make Jess appear.

Billy shifted his weight from foot to foot. I was worried he was going to say something about Jess or May, but all he said was, "Touch a ghost?"

I looked at the ground. "Yeah." I paused. "Do you believe in magic?"

He grinned. "I believe you can do anything if you learn the right tricks." He took my hand from the gazing ball. My breath quickened. We stood there feeling awkward, and then he turned my face towards his and his soft lips brushed mine. He smelled of sweat and wet grass, and his tongue tasted like orange soda. Before I knew it, he was stepping back and looking at me with a sweet smile on his face. "I better go," he said. As he walked across the street, all I could think was, Billy kissed me!

That night we ate dinner on tray tables in front of the TV so we could watch the interview. I was still thinking about Billy's kiss as my parents' pained faces filled the screen. When it was over Dad squeezed Mom's hand, and then the reporter said, "Now, we're going to hear from the boyfriend, Tony Santoro."

"What the hell?" Dad looked at Mom.

Mom let go of his hand. "Maybe it will help."

Dad grimaced as the scene switched to a reporter with a crowd of kids in front of Johnie's. "None of those little bastards would even talk to me when I was there Saturday night looking for her."

Tony was leaning against a car in his jeans and Beatle boots. A curl fell across his forehead, and his pale eyes with their dark lashes made him look sad. Behind him a sign advertised Johnie's

Fat Boy Burgers. Unlike my parents, he wasn't nervous. He acted like the cool guy everyone said he was, dragging the toe of his boot in the dust as he said, "We were having a little party in the desert when this guy pulled up in a red car. I'd never seen him before. He wasn't from around here." He took a haul from his cigarette. "He and Jess got to talking. Before I knew it, she was leaving with him."

"You didn't try to stop her?" The reporter aimed the mike at his face.

"No, I was too mad at her." Tony stubbed out his cigarette. "I was in love with her. We were planning on getting married."

"Married," Dad muttered.

Tony went on, "So I got pretty upset when she told me she was crazy about this dude named Arnie, and that she was running away to be with him, but . . . ." He leaned toward the reporter and said in a loud whisper, "She'd done it before." Dad's eyes almost popped out of his head.

"Done what before?" the reporter asked.

Tony winced. "Fooled around with other guys. I loved Jess, but she had a wild side." He raised his sad eyes to the camera. "It broke my heart when she got in that red car."

The reporter pulled the mike away, saying, "We're going to commercial," and then there was an ad for Tide.

"I've heard enough." Dad shut off the TV. "He had a lot of nerve saying he was going to marry her. I'm going to kill that clown." He rose from his chair.

Mom touched his arm. "Jack, please don't talk that way." When he sat back down she said, "I thought Arnie hadn't heard from her."

"Someone's lying." Dad drank some more scotch.

Mom knotted her hands together. "I can't believe he talked about Jess like that."

I let out a prolonged sigh. Kids at school sometimes said Jess "put out," but she didn't care. She once told me she'd rather be a whore than a puppet-person like Mom, trapped in a little house that she was constantly redecorating because there was nothing else to do.

Dad poured himself and Mom another drink. Soon their voices would get louder. They'd yell. They might cry. They might even hug and talk themselves into a deluded moment of happiness, but I didn't have to watch it.

Jess's black lace bra was still flung on her bureau, where it had been ever since she ran away. I couldn't imagine her wanting to get married, but she and Tony were in love. At least, they used to be. As I picked up her bra I saw a postcard of Schwab's Pharmacy next to it. I remembered sitting there with her while she smiled at herself in the mirror, dreaming of being discovered. When the guy behind the counter told her that Lana Turner actually wasn't discovered there, she became so flustered she almost fell off her stool, but then he'd leaned forward and said, "Sugar, you look more like Lana Turner than anyone I've ever seen." Jess couldn't stop talking about that for days. Mom and Dad were so impressed they couldn't stop talking about it, either.

I turned the postcard over. There was nothing written on it, but I couldn't help but think she'd left it as some kind of message for me.

CHAPTER 6

There'd been some leads since the interview and that was hopeful, but we still hadn't heard from Jess. No phone call. No letters. All I had was a postcard with nothing written on it. I was swimming in the pool to take my mind off things when from behind me someone shouted, "Hey."

I almost lost my lunch. Tony was staring at me from over the fence.

"Sorry, I was hanging out with Deb and heard splashing. I thought it might be . . . ."

"Still missing." I climbed out of the pool.

"This sure isn't easy." He pushed a dark curl off his forehead. "Someday I'll give you some swimming pointers."

I smiled. Tony had been state diving champ before he'd dropped out of school. Jess told me that he didn't even have to practice to win. He just had to picture himself doing a perfect dive. "Come here," he said.

I walked over to the fence, leaving a trail of wet footprints. He looked me up and down, lingering on my purple toenails. "Any more news about Jess?"

"People are seeing her everywhere since you mentioned the red car—Las Vegas, Nogales, New Mexico."

He jutted out his lower lip. "No one believes me, but I know what I'm talking about."

"I know how that feels." I hesitated. "Were you and Jess really getting married?"

"Yeah." There was a faraway look on his face. He was probably thinking of her. "Arnie screwed everything up."

I twisted my wet hair around my hand. "But he says he had no plans to meet her."

He rested his arms on the top of the fence. I could see his muscles. "He's lying."

"But he seemed nice."

"Doesn't mean he is nice. All I know is if they find the red car, they'll find her."

"My parents don't think the police are trying hard enough. They're having a cookout tonight to talk about that with their friends."

"Guess they won't be inviting me." Tony cracked a smile.

I glanced over my shoulder. "They're kind of mad at you right now."

He leaned closer. His lashes were so dark it was like he was wearing mascara. He was in a band, and Jess had told me that all rock-and-roll musicians wore makeup. "I'm going to do some checking around myself. You should, too."

I swallowed hard and said, "I found something out already."

His face sort of twitched. "You did?"

"Jess left a postcard of Schwab's Pharmacy on her bureau. I think it's her way of telling us she's not going to California to see Arnie, that she's following her dreams. You know how much she wants to be a movie star."

"That could make sense." He rubbed his jaw. "You want to come for a ride with me and Deb?"

I clutched my hands together. "I have to go to the cookout."

He looked at me sadly. Blue wasn't a strong enough word for his eyes. They were cerulean. "I'll tell you if I hear anything more about Jess. Hope you'll tell me."

I told him I would, though I wasn't sure about that. Then he reached down, his arm shiny with sweat, and tore a red blossom off the hibiscus bush. His fingers grazed mine as he handed it to me. I stared in awe at the flower on my palm.

"I want you to help me at the cookout tonight, the way you always do, and try to be cheerful. We all need to do that." Mom hesitated, and added, "Margo and Joe are coming, and Ron and Betty Beckham. Betty is bringing May. I thought it might be a chance for the two of you to get to know each other better."

"I do know her, Mom." I sighed. "She's in my class."

"Well, you never talk about her," she said. Of course I didn't talk about her. She was tall and beautiful, with long, straight blonde hair that she was constantly pushing out of her face. Her eyes were a little small, but that didn't mar her perfection. And she was Billy's ex.

Mom and I raced around all afternoon, setting up things for the cookout. I pretended to be excited while we spread a yellow-flowered tablecloth on the picnic table Dad had set up by the pool, and put out pastel-colored napkins and paper plates left over from another party she'd had this summer. But as I gathered up red hibiscus blossoms for a centerpiece, I couldn't stop thinking of Tony handing me the flower, and how strange it felt to be talking to him without Jess there.

Just before the guests arrived, I had to put Dicky to bed. He protested because it was still light out, but soon he was talking to Mr. Rabbit in the quiet singsong voice he used when he was going off into his own little world. When I started to step out, he asked me to wait. He got out of bed, and I followed him into my room and watched as he placed Mr. Rabbit carefully on Jess's pillow. Then he turned to me. "It's a surprise for when she gets back."

"You sure?" I asked. He needed Mr. Rabbit to get to sleep.
He nodded. "I saw her."

"What do you mean?" My voice shook.

"I saw her running."

"Tonight?" I looked hard into his little pointy-chinned face.

He patted Mr. Rabbit's blue head. "No, I saw her in my dream."

I sighed. "Don't worry. You're not the only one who's seeing her. Everyone is."

I hurried over to the bar set up on the patio so I could help make drinks, the way I always did at my parents' parties. Dad stood with his boss Ron and his friend Joe behind a card table cluttered with bottles of liquor and bowls of sliced lemons, limes, cherries, olives, and tiny onions. As I approached, Ron smiled at me, showing his even white teeth, and then turned his attention to the gold watch that gleamed on his tanned wrist.

Joe probably thought he looked cool in his black shirt, but it made him look like a gangster. Mom said he had "connections." It bugged me that she wouldn't just come out and say that he knew people in the Mafia. He and Margo weren't my parents' close friends. Why were they even here?

Dad asked me to make Rob Roys for Mom, Margo, and Betty. It was easy. They were just Manhattans, only with scotch instead of whiskey. I knew a lot about making cocktails, but unlike Jess, I didn't drink them.

I carried the drinks over to the picnic table where Mom was standing with her friends. They all wore pastel-colored dresses. I was wearing a light turquoise one with puff sleeves. May wore a black A-line dress. Lights flickered in the paper lanterns strung around the yard. As the setting sun turned the sky the same pinkish gold as the Rob Roys, Frank Sinatra crooned from the record player Dad had set up in the kitchen. May fiddled with the thin silver bracelet that matched her silver hoop earrings and her silver-circle necklace, and gave me faint smile as I handed her a ginger ale.

Margo held her cigarette out at an angle. "I'm glad some good has come of the interview, in spite of those awful things Tony said."

Betty leaned close. "My Linda says you can't believe a word that comes out of that boy's mouth. Can't understand what any girl would see in him."

Mom flinched. "You know teens."

Betty lit a cigarette. "Any news about Arnie?"

Mom shook her head. "He hasn't heard from Jess. But with all these sightings, you've got to wonder." She paused. "Just this morning, someone thought they saw Jess in Nogales."

Margo widened her turquoise-shadowed eyes. "I hear you can get married for around twenty dollars down there."

"Tony's probably on his way there to marry her right now." Betty smirked.

Mom looked stricken. I pushed myself forward. I had to tell them. "Tony isn't on his way there. I talked to him this morning, and he misses Jess as much as any of us."

"You were talking to him?" Mom was staring at me like I'd done something awful. Everyone was, even May. "Just stay away from Tony, and let us handle this." She handed me a red plastic bowl from the table. "Go refill the chips, please."

Cradling the bowl in my arms like something absurdly precious, I went into the kitchen, dumped an entire bag of chips into it, and stuffed a whole bunch into my mouth. How could they talk about Tony that way? If it weren't for him, there would be no leads. He was the one who'd actually gotten people's attention during the interview, the one who mentioned the red car. Even I could see that his dark-lashed eyes didn't have a speck of meanness in them.

He'd seemed so sad when I talked to him by the pool. He was probably agonizing right now over letting Jess slip through his fingers that night. I thought of the huge fight they'd had when we got back from California. Tony had called and asked to come over, but Jess was mad at him for flirting with some girl. He was always flirting. She went on and on about how Arnie was so much nicer, and a better kisser. And then I'm pretty sure she said, "I did it with him."

Tony yelled, "You bitch," so loud I could hear him through the phone.

Then she shouted, "It's over," and told him she didn't want to see him ever again.

Later, the bell rang while we were in the bedroom. She opened the window and leaned out. He looked up and said, "You know you love me, Jez-e-bell."

She told him to go away, but he didn't. The door was unlocked, and he let himself in. We heard him pounding up the stairs. Before Jess could say a word, he was holding her in his arms.

"So you don't want to see me." He gripped her chin. She tried to struggle free, but he wouldn't let her. As he pushed his mouth against hers, the hard curve of his biceps made me feel squirmy inside. They kissed and he said he was sorry if he held her too tight, it was just that he loved her so much he didn't know his own strength.

He was so beautiful. When they finished kissing, Jess said she'd only said those things to make him jealous. She loved him more than life itself. It was like I wasn't even in the room. I was deciding that love makes other people invisible, and making a mental note to write this down in case it turned out to be brilliant, when

Tony turned to me and said, "Like what you see, Twinkle Toes?"
I blushed to the roots of my hair.

Maybe Tony wasn't the perfect boyfriend, but there was something special between them. You just had to be around them to feel it. It didn't make sense that Jess would take off and leave him for Arnie or to follow her dreams. Something must have gone terribly wrong.

CHAPTER 7

After dinner, everyone drifted inside for dessert, coffee, and more drinks, but I stayed by the pool. May was ignoring me, and I was tired of listening to my parents' crappy conversations. So much had happened—Billy's kiss, Tony handing me the flower, my sister gone—and I didn't understand any of it. I was considering making *myself* a Rob Roy when the sliding door opened. Mom walked out with Ron. They stood in front of the orange tree with drinks in their hands. Ron raised his martini.

"I miss her." Mom leaned her head on his shoulder.

"This may be hard to hear, but you need to hire a private eye." He touched her hair, a sad smile on his face. "I know someone good."

"Jack doesn't want to hire one," Mom said. "You know he has to do everything himself."

"Then we'll have to make him want to." He slid his hand along her cheek and tilted her face toward his. I was holding myself so still I thought I might crack.

"Frannie," he said. He wrapped his arms around her. The sound of her crying softly into his shirt made me ill. He pushed her hair away from her face, kissed her on the forehead, and then by her ear. I hated the way he called her Frannie. No one called her that.

Mom was in the kitchen with Betty and Margo cleaning up when I came back inside. "Where were you?" she asked.

I could barely look at her. I muttered, "Nowhere," and then she told May and me to see if the guys wanted more drinks. At the edge of the living room, May put her finger to her lips. Ron was trying to convince Dad to hire the private eye. Dad nodded without going along just like Mom said he would, because he really didn't trust anyone else to do anything. No one could load the dishwasher right. No one else knew how to drive properly. And no one could find Jess, even though he'd already failed so miserably.

Ron flicked his cigarette into the maple-leaf-shaped ashtray I'd made in elementary school. "Jack, the police have decided she's a runaway. That means they've stopped looking. Just have a talk with this guy."

Dad gazed into the smoky depths of his scotch, as if searching for an answer. "If that's what I have to do, I guess I will."

Then Joe started talking about having Tony beaten up if nothing else worked, and I thought I might faint. What was going on? It was like they were all ganging up on Tony and heading off in the wrong direction. And really, no one knew what was going on, except maybe me, because I'd been thinking about this. Logically. Leaving May standing there, I ran up to my room, got the postcard and hurried back downstairs. I cleared my throat as I handed it to Dad.

"What is this, honey?" His breath reeked of alcohol.

"It's a postcard of Schwab's Pharmacy that I found on Jess's bureau. I think she's letting us know she's going to Hollywood to become a movie star." Everyone was watching me. "Maybe you should tell that to the private eye, and he can look for her there."

"Little pitchers have big ears." Joe grinned.

Dad eyed me sternly. "The things we're talking about here have nothing to do with you, Caroline."

"But I know it's a message from her." I felt desperate and excited at the same time.

"Message?" Dad turned the postcard over. "I don't see anything." He was looking at me like I was some kind of nut. Everyone was. And maybe I was. I ran out of the room, through the sliding glass doors, and out to the pool.

I was dumping scotch and vermouth into a silver cocktail shaker when May walked over. She slipped a red flower from the centerpiece behind her ear and said, "Can I have some of that?" I smiled. At least she was finally talking to me.

I poured a glass for each of us and we sat down by the edge of the pool. Lights in the paper lanterns glowed like small fuzzy suns in the darkness. The only sound was the lapping of the water around our bare feet.

I took a big sip of my drink, and coughed. "Not sure I like this."

"You'll get used to it," May said, "and then it will be fun."

I guzzled some more, and it burned all the way down. "What a boring party."

"Everything's boring. Even Billy." She averted her gaze. She must have broken up with him and not the other way around, but I wasn't about to ask. I wondered if she knew anything about her dad and my mom, but couldn't imagine asking about that either. She sipped her drink and went on, "What your dad said when you showed him the postcard was mean. You were only trying to help."

"He wouldn't even listen to me." The burning was now a warmth in my chest.

"I hate the way adults think they know everything and we don't know anything. They never listen." Reflections wavered on the water, touching and parting silently. She pushed her pale, silky hair from her face. "Do you really think Jess is in California?"

"That's what Tony and his friends say."

"My sister Linda told me that, too." She drank some more.

"She knows Tony?"

"Everyone knows him. He's a legend."

"'Cause he has all those parties?"

"No. He's the kid who couldn't die. Don't you know that?"

I nodded. "Jess told me something about it, but not the whole story."

"When Tony was in sixth grade, we got so much rain there were rivers in the desert. He went swimming in one with his friends and got swept away. When they found him, they thought he was dead. But on the way to the morgue, one of his eyes twitched. If no one had noticed he might have been buried alive. It was in the paper. They called him the miracle boy." She smiled. "Later he became a state diving champ. Strange, huh?"

I took another big gulp and said, "Jess told me that when Tony died he walked in the darkness, and when he came back to life that darkness gave him special powers, like seeing things before they happen." I looked up at her, figuring she'd be impressed.

She rolled her eyes. "Yeah, and some kids think he can never die."

I dipped my hand in the pool. "Do you think he can die?"

"Of course. We all die." She stared at me. "You can't believe everything everyone tells you."

"I don't," I said, though I wanted to believe in things like that.

We drank some more, and after a while it didn't taste so bad. May curled up on the tiles next to the pool. As she trailed her hand in the water she said, "I'm really sorry about what happened to Jess. It must be so hard for you." Her words sent a chill through me. She was talking like something terrible had already happened. Everyone was saying things like that, and I hated it.

My feet looked pale under the water, almost as if they didn't belong to me—as if they belonged to a drowned person. For a second, I had this creepy feeling I wasn't in my own body. "I wish I could do something to help find her," I said, "but everyone acts like I'm just in the way."

She propped herself up on an elbow. "Don't be silly. Just because adults don't want to listen doesn't mean there's nothing you can do. They don't know everything. We see things and hear things they miss." I wondered if she was right, if I really could do something. She took the flower from behind her ear and dropped it in the water. "And we know things we don't tell."

"Do you?" I asked.

"Everyone does." She turned her gaze to the moon, high and white in the sky. Clouds sailed past it. A faint breeze brushed my ear. The red flower bobbed on the water.

"Tony gave me a flower just like that," I said.

Her small eyes widened. "When?"

"This morning. He's really sad about Jess."

Her expression became serious. "You should stay away from him. Linda says you never know what will happen with him and those kids he hangs out with."

I leaned forward. "You mean at those parties he has in the guesthouse?"

She nodded knowingly.

The sliding door opened and her mom called out that they were leaving. May walked over to her with surprising steadiness, one foot in front of the other like something she'd learned in charm school, and with a flick of her wrist she clicked the door shut.

I stumbled onto the chaise longue. It felt like the backyard was some mad carousel going around, and then I tasted puke at the back of my throat and everything inside me came up. As vomit flowed across the tiles, I shut my eyes. In that darkness I saw Jess in a tiny movie in my head. She looked like a Barbie doll, wearing sunglasses smaller than thumbnails, a red bikini, raising a tiny plastic hand, and as she waved, behind her another Jess appeared, even smaller and more doll-like, and behind her another and another, and with each new Jess there was a plink sound like ice cubes in a glass. They were stepping stones extending into infinite darkness until she was a speck, small as a distant star, and it was like she was going further and further away, but it was reassuring because at least she was somewhere, and I was seeing her, even if it was only in my head.

Whoosh. I opened my eyes to see Dad hosing down the tiles. I expected him to yell but all he said was, "Looks like we have a case of upchuck here." The stink of puke filled the air. He swayed on his feet. "I'm going to California to look for Jess, and I'll make sure to stop by Schwab's. I can see her doing something crazy like going to Hollywood all by herself."

CHAPTER 8

The next day I stood with Mom and Dicky on the front step, watching Dad leave for California.

As he drove away, Mom said, "I don't understand how he can leave me here at a time like this." She gave me a look and headed back into the house, obviously in a mood. She'd started in on me at breakfast by slamming around the kitchen. Each slam made my head hurt. When I couldn't eat my scrambled eggs, she'd said, "Feeling a little sick? It's called a hangover."

She went into the living room and sat down at the sewing machine. Pieces of yellow cloth were strewn all over the rug. She pressed the pedal with her foot, and the needle pounded into the fabric at breakneck speed. When she finished a panel she held it up against the picture window. Sunlight streamed through the material, illuminating the pale buttercups printed on it. She stared out, crumpling the cloth in her hand.

A sour taste filled my mouth. "Dad will find her. I know he will."

Mom just stood there. "None of us knows anything."

I thought of Ron's hand softly brushing her cheek, how she pressed her face into his shirt. And of finding the postcard and Dad finally listening to me, and of the things May said by the pool. Mom was wrong. I was starting to know things. I knew that Jess had probably taken off to pursue her dreams. But I also knew that she and Tony were in love. They had known it from the moment they first saw each other. She'd said though it seemed accidental, it was fate.

It *was* kind of accidental. Last fall, right after we'd moved here, Mom dropped us off at a public swimming pool because ours was being cleaned. Jesse wore her red bikini that fastened in front with a rose. I wore my black-and-white one.

As we inhaled the moist, chlorine-scented air, she'd nodded toward a boy climbing the stairs to the high dive. His dark hair was combed back from his face, and he was slim with broad, square shoulders. He placed his feet together, raised his muscled arms above his head, stood still to let the crowd admire him, and dove. The diving board made a springing sound as he sailed through the air and cut into the green water like a pale knife. When he emerged with a splash, everyone clapped. As he hoisted himself out of the pool, he stared straight at Jess.

A girl in the crowd turned to us. It was Debbie Frank.

"So what'd ya think of Tony?" she said.

Jess looked off to the side. "I guess he's good."

Debbie touched the spit curl plastered to her cheek. "He's more than good. He was state diving champ."

Before Jess could make some wise remark, Tony came over. Up close he looked like one of those Greek statues, only wet. Just a glimpse of his deep-set blue eyes made me shiver. He draped his arm around Debbie's shoulder. "Who are these two angels?"

Debbie introduced us and Tony fixed his eyes on Jess and said, "Hi there." She fiddled with the rose on her suit. They stared at each other in one of those moments that are uncomfortable and impossible to ignore.

Finally Tony broke his stare, and said he had to go. As he walked away, he turned slowly, pointed at Jess, and said, "See you around."

"He's *my* boyfriend," Debbie said when he was gone.

Jess widened her eyes. "Really?"

"Don't act like that's so hard to believe," Debbie said.

Later Jess confided in me that when she first saw Tony, he had the loneliest look she'd ever seen. She said that the darkness from when he almost drowned set him apart from everyone. Then she'd leaned close as if it were a very special secret, and whispered, "And when our eyes met, his loneliness became a part of me. It was love."

Remembering the history of their love was reassuring. Even someone as stuck on herself as Jess wouldn't just run way from Tony and never come back.

I spent Sunday afternoon waiting for Dad to come home from California. He'd called a few times over the past week but never with any news, and I was starting to worry, but I hadn't given up hope. Ron came by once to consult with Mom about the private eye. Consult seemed to be a code word for drinking martinis until their voices slurred together. I wished I could ask Jess about Mom and Ron. I couldn't stop my imagination from running wild, and Jess understood people so much better than I did.

As I sat on my bed, waiting, I picked up my book. There were only a few days left to finish it before school started, but I was almost done. It wasn't as exciting as I'd imagined it would be, but I liked the parts where the author talked about taking peyote, a cactus that grew in the desert—how weird was that? When he took it, mostly he stared at ordinary things like the folds in his pants and saw them in a new and beautiful way. But it wasn't just the outside world that changed. Peyote could transport you to a part of the mind that he called the antipodes. It was like a forgotten neighborhood you never knew was there. Sometimes people saw jewels, islands of flowers, and magical beings; other times, things that were terrifying. It made me think of the vision

I'd had inside my head of Jess by the pool. Did it come from the antipodes? But if it did, why was Jess *there*? It had to be some kind of sign that I was on the right path, though I had no idea where it would lead me.

When I came downstairs, Dad was sitting at the kitchen table with Mom and Dicky, and no Jess. My chair scraped against the floor as I yanked it out and sat down. Dad gave me a sad smile and reached into a plastic bag by his chair. "I stopped by the souvenir shop where Arnie works." He handed Dicky a plastic Mickey Mouse hat, me a ruby-slipper keychain, and Mom a green bracelet.

She eyed it suspiciously. "It's nice for costume jewelry."

"A little bit of the Emerald City," he said. Mom slipped it on. He let out a long breath. "I found out Arnie has a girlfriend. He and Jess were just flirting. There was nothing between them."

Mom fussed with the tablecloth. "I'd been hoping she'd run off with him." She looked toward the window over the sink. Dicky put the hat on and began moving his face from side to side in front of hers. "Stop that," she said, pushing him away. She glanced at Dad. "Did you find anything else out?"

He flicked his beer cap off the table. "I walked all over Hollywood. I went to places where runaway kids crash on dirty mattresses. Some of them were on drugs. Some of the girls looked like prostitutes. They were all full of stupid ideas about dropping out and being free, but none of them had seen Jess." He wiped his forehead with a napkin and went on, "I saw a girl on Redondo Beach, wearing a red bathing suit just like Jess's. I followed her. She started to run. I ran, too. I'd almost caught up with her when she turned around and screamed. It wasn't Jess. Not even close. Everyone was staring at me like I was some kind of pervert." He slumped in his seat. "I tried as hard as I could, but all I accomplished was scaring some teenage girl. I'm lucky I didn't get arrested."

Mom touched his arm. "You did your best. That's what matters."

He pulled his arm away. "Easy for you to say. You're not the one who told her never to come back."

She placed her hands on the table and lowered her voice. "Ron thinks Tony might know something about the disappearance of Geraldine Keanen." I caught my breath. I remembered when that happened.

Dad gave her an agonized look. "Isn't she the girl who went missing last fall?"

She nodded. I tried to swallow, but I couldn't. Geraldine had been in Jess's class. The newspaper said it was like she'd vanished into thin air. People talked about it for weeks, and then they stopped.

He tore at the label on his beer bottle. "I guess we have to hope Ron is wrong."

"Joe's friends are going to put some pressure on Tony," Mom said. "They'll get him to talk."

"What?" Dad sat up straighter. "Was anyone going to ask me about this?"

She turned the bracelet round on her wrist. "Ron thought it was a good idea."

"Ron? Did it ever occur to Ron or Joe that strong-arming Tony and his friends might not be the best way to get them to talk to us?"

Mom frowned. "Then what should we do, Jack?"

"There isn't anything we can do. Her friends might know more than they're saying. Tony might know more. But they don't trust us. They'll only talk to each other. We've gone as far as we can." He took a long swallow of beer. "Our only hope is that a kid with some decency will come forward." His shoulders sagged like he'd given up. I couldn't let that happen. I'd found the postcard. I'd had a vision.

"Dad," I said, "you went to Schwab's Pharmacy, right?"

"Schwab's?" He stared at me blankly.

"You didn't go there?"

He started to say, "I meant to . . . ."

Of course he'd forgotten. No one ever listened to me. And they didn't get it. Jess wasn't some grimy runaway. She was obsessed with getting what she wanted. She always had been. "Dad," I said, "I still think Jess is in California. We just have to look harder for her, because she ran away to become a star. And she doesn't care how much that hurts us, because she only cares about herself."

Mom grimaced. "Caroline, how can you talk about your sister that way?"

"Because it's the truth."

CHAPTER 9

May called on the day before school started and invited me to go shopping with her and her best friend Sheila. As I brushed Jess's blue mascara down to the tips of my lashes, Mom walked into my room. I glanced at her uneasily. We'd hardly talked since Dad got back. The two of them fought all the time now.

"I'm glad you're doing something with May today," she said. "It's good to distract yourself." She reached into a satin makeup bag on the bureau and took out some light green eye shadow.

"Try this color." She stepped back. "I always thought your eyes were hazel, but they're more unusual. They remind me of this stone called tiger's eye." Tiger's eye, I thought, as if she had given me some rare clue as to who I was. She handed me some money and gazed at me sadly, as if I was the one who was missing.

May and Sheila were best friends, but they weren't much alike. Sheila had frizzy brown hair. She wasn't as pretty as May, but she had a clean, pale look and she worshipped May, as most people did. I was anxious for the three of us to become friends, and also for the chance to ask May more about Jess.

When we got to the store, I chose a sleeveless mini-dress with black and white squares on top, and red and white ones on the bottom, and shoes with chunky heels and tiny dots on the toes. They were exactly like May's, only in black patent leather instead of suede, but if she minded she didn't say so. Sheila bought a low-cut dress that showed off her cleavage, and May bought a black hip-hugger skirt that Sheila said looked amazing with her long legs. May hated being tall, and Sheila tried hard to make her feel better about it.

When we were done shopping, we took the bus to Speedway Boulevard to get something to eat. We stopped at a place called The Flying Saucer.

"Johnie's is much better," I said. "Tony hates this place. He says he wouldn't waste his time at a second-rate place, with second-rate people, and waiters dressed like the creature from the black lagoon."

Sheila and May exchanged an awkward glance. May swept her long hair off her shoulder. It fell in a shiny straight sheet, perfectly even at the bottom, milk-pale strands blending in with slightly lighter and darker ones.

"I love your hair," I said.

May smiled. "Anyone can have this color. It's called Ivory Chiffon."

Then Sheila said she would die of hunger if we waited a minute longer, so we went in and sat down in a booth covered with fake alligator skin, and ordered Alien Burgers, Pluto Fries, and Saturn's O-Rings from a waiter in a lizard suit.

I was preparing to ask May more about what she'd told me by the pool when she took a tiny bite of her burger and said, "Billy called me last night." My stomach lurched.

Sheila tapped a nail coated with clear polish on the table. "What did you talk about?"

"About Steve being in Vietnam." She hunched her shoulders as if trying to appear shorter.

I said, "He talked to me about Steve, too."

The two of them turned to me. "He did?"

"Yeah. We talked about how hard it was with Steve and Jess being gone." I tore the paper off my straw. "And then he kissed me."

Sheila blinked her dark eyes. "He kissed you?"

I nodded. May shot me a look. "Billy's been a mess since we broke up. He calls me every night. And he's drinking too much." She licked her glossy pink lips. "He's doing all kinds of crazy things."

I pushed my plate aside. Billy hadn't spoken to me since the kiss, but apparently he was talking to May all the time. I had some fries left, but I'd lost my appetite. When the lizard waiter asked if anyone wanted dessert, I was relieved that no one did. I couldn't wait to leave.

As we handed the cashier our money, she said, "You girls be careful. It's getting dark out." May and Sheila suppressed a giggle. The cashier looked up at us with sad eyes, her skin pasty and damp-looking, clusters of fake silver pearls dangling from her ears. "You might think this is funny but my Geraldine, she never came home. There's not a night I don't leave a light on for her."

I froze. Geraldine. The cashier stared straight at me, as if she knew my sister was missing just like Geraldine was, and saw right through my pathetic attempt to be happy. May grabbed my wrist and pulled me away.

When we were outside, May turned to me. "I'm sorry. I forgot she worked there." She added in a whisper, "My sister and Geraldine were in some of the same classes. Linda said she was smart and interested in fish."

"Marine biology," Sheila said. She cupped her hands around her lips. "Some kids say that she was murdered, and that her spirit walks the desert."

"What?" It felt like the air was rushing out of me. "Who's saying that?"

May glared at Sheila. "Linda says those are just rumors."

First Mom mentioning Geraldine, and now rumors I'd never heard. There was so much I didn't know. "I need to talk to them."

"No, you don't," May said. "They're really bad news. And there's no such thing as spirits." She glanced over her shoulder. "Please don't blab this around. Linda told us not to tell anyone, and we're only telling you because of what happened to Jess."

What happened to Jess? I got the awful taste of onion rings in my mouth. Black shreds of darkness floated in the air. It was like all their whispers were tearing me apart, and at any moment I was going to faint. "We better get going. Mom will kill me if I'm late," I said.

Speedway grew livelier as we waited for the bus. Cars full of kids cruised by. Some slowed and boys called out to us. Everyone was out looking for someone or something. I gripped my bag tightly. Soon the night would close over us, and this would be Jess's world—the world we'd lost her in.

It felt like the bus would never come. I was relieved when Tony pulled up in his gold car and rolled down the window. "You girls want a ride home?"

I looked from May to Sheila. May mouthed, *No.*

"Thank you, but we're taking the bus," I said.

Tony sighed. "Caroline, this is Speedway. Any minute the rattlesnakes will be slithering out of the woodwork. You really want to wait for the bus?"

I looked at May again. She shrugged.

"If you really don't mind," I said.

Tony smiled. "It will be my pleasure."

They sat in back while I sat in front. The car smelled like my parents' house after a party—"eau de cigarettes and stale beer." I kicked aside some paper cups on the floor and put my bags down by my feet.

"You buy some nice stuff?" Tony fiddled with the radio.

"School clothes," I replied.

"Three little schoolgirls," he said, and I could feel May and Sheila holding back laughter. "Jess always said you loved to study." The car became silent.

"I suppose I do," I said.

As he drove fast with one hand on the wheel, the other reaching for a cigarette, he said, "Light that for me, hon." I beamed, hoping Sheila and May had heard, and lit his cigarette and handed it back to him. "Thanks, I needed that," he said, exhaling. "You girls want a smoke?"

"No thanks," Sheila said.

"Not even you, May? I could have sworn you were the sophisticated French actress type."

She stared into her hands and didn't answer. He took a curve so fast I was pushed up against him. "Whoa," he said. "Sorry about that, sugar." He patted my arm with his free hand. When we got to May's house he said, "It sure was nice meeting you, hon."

I was jealous that he called her hon, too, but all she did was frown and say, "Thanks for the ride."

"I'm getting out here, too," Sheila said.

Tony grinned. "You two sisters?"

"No, I'm just hanging out at her house." I waited for May to invite me too, but she didn't.

Tony eyed them.

"Yeah, you don't look a bit like sisters."

I watched as they disappeared into May's house. As we drove down her dark, curving street, it felt strange now that it was just the two of us in the car. He turned to me. "You'd be as pretty as May if you were blonde, prettier maybe."

Though I knew this was just flattery, I couldn't stop smiling.

"There's a party at my place tonight. My band's gonna play," he added.

"I'm late. I should have been home hours ago."

"Don't worry, chickadee. I'm not inviting you."

I felt foolish for thinking he was. As he blew a stream of smoke out the window, I took the box with my new patent leather shoes out of the bag at my feet.

"What have you got there?" he asked.

"New shoes." I lifted the lid and beheld their shiny loveliness, pristine as a frozen pond back east before a single skate had touched it. I missed winter so much. Here, the closest thing to snow was the cold stars that sprinkled the sky. I felt a catch in my throat. What if I never saw snow again? Or Jess?

Tony rested his arm on the back of my seat. "Jess never liked going to parties with me." It was as if he'd known I was thinking about her. He went on, "She wanted me all to herself. She didn't understand I need to have a lot of other people around, but that's not important now. Nothing is the same anymore." I followed his gaze out the window. We were in my neighborhood. I'd been down this street many times, but it was like I was seeing the inky palm fronds and soft glow of the streetlights for the first time. Tony was right. Nothing was the same.

I put the box back in my shopping bag. "Sometimes I think it's my fault she's missing." He glanced at me. "If I'd told Mom right away when she snuck out, they would have looked for her sooner. She might be here right now." I slouched in my seat.

"And I thought everyone blamed me," Tony said. He laughed as though my confession was really nothing, and I was relieved. He pulled up about a block from my house and said, "If your parents saw me dropping you off, they'd kill me. They don't understand how much I want to find Jess."

I looked down at my hands. "They don't."

"Caroline." His voice made me jump. "Look here." He leaned close and pointed to a dull purple bruise on his face. "You know how I got that?" I shook my head. He pressed my hand to his cheek. I could almost feel how much it hurt. "One of your dad's friends. I got other bruises. You want to see?" He began to lift his shirt.

"No." I winced. "I'm sorry they did that to you."

"They think I know something about Geraldine Keanen. Don't know how they got that idea. Do you?"

My stomach tightened. "Probably some stupid rumor kids are spreading."

"Jesus, I hardly knew the girl."

I was glad to hear that. "Everyone's got crazy ideas," I said.

"That private eye your dad sent sure asked a lot of questions."

"My dad didn't send him. His boss Ron did."

"Well, you might want to tell Ron to stop asking me questions and actually start looking for Jess."

I sighed. "My dad went to California to look for her, but he didn't find out anything. He didn't even go to Schwab's."

"Unbelievable. That's the most important thing he could have done."

I smiled. "That's just what I thought."

He glanced at himself in the rearview mirror. "Everyone blames me and you, but sometimes I think we're the only ones who really want to find her."

"I know what you mean," I said. "It's like my parents have already given up."

"That's how some people are when something bad happens. Their fear paralyzes them." He was staring at me, his eyes so blue they seemed to jump out of his face. I wanted to look away, but I couldn't move. It was almost as if *I* was paralyzed.

He cocked his head. "But you and me, we're not like most people."

I twirled some hair around my finger. He'd seen death and come back from it, and I'd had a vision of my sister. We'd both been touched by something from outside of this world. Maybe we were alike.

He went on, "I think we can find Jess."

I felt hopeful for the first time in a while. "How?"

He shook his head. "As soon as I come up with a plan, I'll let you know."

I hesitated. "I've got to go. I'm going to get in trouble for being late."

He smiled. "Just tell them the bus broke down."

CHAPTER 10

The next day at school, in every one of my classes as attendance was taken, the teacher would pause extra long after I said, "Here," wondering, I suppose, what to say to the girl whose sister had disappeared. Kids I knew from last year kept their distance. Kids I didn't know didn't approach me. All I wanted was to be anywhere other than this place where everyone stopped talking as soon as I came near them. By the time I got to AP English, my last class of the day, I was officially sick of school.

Everyone turned to look when May walked in. She gave me an embarrassed smile as she sat down next to me, and angled her long legs to one side. "I know I don't really belong here. My mom got the principal to let me in." She pushed her curtain of hair out of her face. "So were your parents mad when you got home last night?"

I shrugged. "I told them the bus broke down."

Our teacher, Mr. Raymond, wore a wrinkled plaid shirt and looked like he'd forgotten to comb his hair, but all the kids liked him. Even Jess did. She said he let kids talk about real stuff like rock-and-roll, love, and what was wrong with the world. He handed out copies of poems by E.E. Cummings and asked us each to choose one to read aloud. We would have one minute and not a second more to give our impression. The only wrong answer was silence.

The words in the poems were all mashed together. Lines zigzagged across the page and there was no punctuation. It was like

E.E. Cummings was saying screw the world, I can write however I want. I was so entranced, for a second I forgot about Jess. When I saw the phrase "blue-eyed boy" in one of the poems, I made my choice. Class was almost over before it was my turn. As I read, "How do you like your blueeyed boy Mister Death," the room grew quiet. Everyone was staring at me, curious as to what the girl whose sister was probably dead would say about death. "It's . . . ." No words came. Silence was the wrong answer.

Mr. Raymond cocked his head. "Are you all right?"

This was the worst. I wasn't all right. There was an impossible tickle in my throat. "Buffalo Bill did everything fast, riding the water-smooth stallion, breaking onetwothreefourfive pigeonsjustlikethat. He was impatient for life. But now Mister Death has him, and he's . . . ." I could barely get the word out. "Still." The blank faces in front of me blurred.

At the end of class, Mr. Raymond gave a homework assignment to write a poem inspired by the one we'd read aloud. As May and I were leaving, he motioned to me. I braced myself for his uncomfortable words of concern.

He tucked in a shirttail. "If you ever want to talk about poetry or anything else, I want you to know I'll listen." I nodded and rushed past him.

The corridor was nearly empty. I'd missed my chance to do something with May or Sheila after school. As I grabbed some books from my locker, someone tapped me on the shoulder and I almost dropped them. I turned to see Billy standing behind me.

He said, "You walking home?"

Buffalo Bill, Billy—reality stranger than a poem. I hadn't seen him since the kiss. Talk to him, I thought. Now. Before he leaves. "Yes."

"Want to walk home together?" he asked.

As we stepped out into the sunlight-soaked world, Tony's gold car was idling in front of the school. He was everywhere lately. For a moment I thought he was waiting for me, but then Debbie came over and got in.

May and Sheila walked up to us, and May beamed at Billy and said, "Linda's picking us up. She can give you a ride home." She added, "And you, too, Caroline."

Billy shook his head. "No, thanks. I need the exercise."

May frowned. "Caroline, you can still come if you want."

"That's okay. I need the exercise, too." I tried to look disappointed I wasn't going with her.

For a moment, she was at a loss for words. Then Linda pulled up in a bright red convertible. "Last chance, guys," she said. "Top down."

Billy smiled. "Maybe another time." As they sped away, Billy shook his head. "May doesn't like to hear 'no.'"

As we walked, circles of sweat formed under my armpits. My dress was plastered to my back, and my shoes hurt. More than anything I wanted a cold drink, but there weren't any stores, just house after house, all the same, right down to their brown front lawns with prickly cacti rising out of the dust.

When we were in front of his house, I said, "Thank God. I can't take another step."

"If my bike wasn't broken, I wouldn't be walking," Billy said.

"Your bike is broken?"

"Yeah. I wiped out coming home from a party at a dry wash in the desert."

"What were you doing at one of those parties?" Jess had told me about how kids liked to hang out and drink in the dry creek beds in the desert.

"Drinking," Billy said. "Don't look so surprised, Caroline. Everyone drinks." He wiped some sweat from his brow. "Can I ask you a question?"

I smiled, waiting for something romantic. "Okay."

"I was wondering how you're dealing with it."

My heart sank when I realized he was talking about my sister, but I gave him the advice people always gave me. "I just put it out of my mind and go on. What else is there to do?"

"Right." Billy paused. "We got a letter from Steve yesterday." He let out a slow sigh. "He saw someone get his head blown off. It's good to hear from him, but I wouldn't want to know if something like that happened to Steve. I'd rather go on thinking he's all right." He looked at me. "Is that how you feel about Jess?"

For a second I couldn't speak.

"I wish I had a letter from her," I finally said. "It could say, 'I hate you all' or 'I'm never coming back,' it wouldn't matter. Just hearing from her would be enough. Not knowing is the worst." My stomach was in a knot. "She could be a pain, but it's a bummer not having her around."

"I always assumed Steve would be here to watch my games." His face stiffened. "This war is ruining everything. My dad will kill me, but if it's still going on when I graduate, I'm going to Canada."

I looked at him in disbelief. "And run away like Jess?"

"Caroline," he said. He kicked a stone into the gutter. It clattered when it hit the bottom. "I meant to tell you a while ago, but I didn't know how. That party I mentioned was on the night your sister went missing."

"Did you see her?" My heart was beating like a mad butterfly.

He sighed. "It was dark and I was drunk. I didn't see her there."

"Did you see a red car or anything that seemed strange? Try to remember. Even the smallest detail could help."

He pushed his hand through his hair. "I'm trying to remember. I wish I hadn't been so drunk." He stared at me a moment too long. I wondered if he was about to kiss me. He started to say, "There was something," but then stopped. Linda's car drew up to the curb. May and Sheila got out and came over to us.

"What's going on, guys?" May clasped her hands in front of her. I glanced at Billy. "We were talking about Jess."

She leaned into him and whispered, "Don't you go scaring Caroline with more stupid rumors." Then she took his arm and the three of them headed toward his house. She asked if I was coming, but I told her no.

I'd hardly gotten through our front door before Mom was breathing down my neck, shouting, "I can't believe what you did."

"What did I do?" I asked cautiously.

"Betty Beckham just called." She sighed. "I know you lied about last night. Betty told me. The bus didn't break down and I don't know what's worse—the fact that you got a ride home from Tony, or that you lied about it."

I glanced away. "I only said that because I knew you'd be more worried if I told the truth."

"The truth? So tell me, Caroline, what is the truth?"

All I wanted to do was leave the room but she wasn't about to let that happen. "Mom, the bus was really late and Speedway was creepy, so we let Tony drive us home."

"That's not what Betty told me. She said May wanted to wait for the bus, but you insisted on the ride from Tony. And now she thinks you're a bad influence on May. Do you have any idea how embarrassing that is for me?"

"That's not true." I wondered why May had said that. Was she mad because Billy walked me home?

"And I should believe you over Betty? You?" She stood there, looking wronged, in front of the yellow buttercup-splattered curtains that she'd managed to finish in spite of everything going on.

"Go ahead, believe her if you want. You don't care about me. You don't even care that Jess is missing. And you don't care about Betty, either. You only care about Ron." The words just slipped out.

She gasped. "What are you talking about? Is something wrong with you?" She was staring at me as if she was convinced I was the worst person in the world. She went on, "Really, I'm worried you're becoming a pathological liar."

"Mom," I said, "I saw you and Ron on the patio."

"So now you're spying on me?"

"I wasn't spying on you. I was outside by the pool."

"Ron and I were just talking. He was comforting me. God knows, no one else does. You have no idea how hard this all is."

I flinched.

She went on, "That's all it was, no matter what your twisted mind tells you."

"Okay, Mom," I said.

"It's not okay." She grabbed my arm. "You lied and you put yourself in danger. Don't you think I have enough to worry about?" I wouldn't look at her. "You are never, ever to have anything to do with Tony again. Do you understand that?"

I bit my lip. "I do understand. I understand that he wants to find my sister. What's wrong with that? Tony said Schwab's Pharmacy was important, but Dad didn't even bother to go there. Both of you just want to drink and forget about her."

She stared at me as if I was the greatest disappointment on earth.

I went upstairs and slammed my door, hoping she heard. It would serve my parents right if I never spoke to them again. But none of this was as bad as May telling on me for going with Tony.

I hadn't told on Jess for going off with Tony the night she disappeared. I thought I was doing the right thing—what anyone

I knew would have done. It was so hard to know what the right thing to do was.

As I sat and thought, a poem for the assignment came to me and I hurried to write it down before I lost the inspiration. After a few tries I had this:

Death and the Buttercup

Death ~~flash~~smash the buttercup
In a moment
Brief as yellow ~~pollen~~FLOWERBLOOD
Under your chin,
Death steps in,
And ~~she is~~you are magicanddisappearing
Gone!

I went over to the window and peered down at the street. There were streets running parallel to ours, and more streets beyond those. All over the world there were streets and Jess might be on any one of them, reaching down to buckle her shoe, pushing her hair behind her ear, smiling at a stranger. She was *somewhere*, and if she was somewhere she could be found. I'd always assumed that even if no one else could, Dad would find her. But Dad had given up. Everyone had.

A red car stopped in front of Billy's house. My hand went to my throat, but it was just Linda again. May came outside with Sheila and Billy. They whispered to each other. Sheila glanced my way but didn't see me. I pushed up the window, but I still couldn't hear them. What were they talking about? Geraldine? About something Billy remembered from the party? My stomach twisted as they drove away. Dad had said we had to wait for a decent kid to come forward. But kids didn't talk to parents—they talked to other kids.

I felt something soft as I pressed my hands down on the sill. It was a dead moth, all gray and powdery. I screamed, frantically brushing it off my palm.

I took slow, deep breaths. They were going somewhere now, laughing at jokes I couldn't hear. But soon I would hear. I would listen to everything they said, and make them tell me their secrets. I turned away from the window. Maybe it was up to me to find my sister.

CHAPTER 11

The next day at lunch, I sat down at a table with May, Sheila, and Billy. They all stared at me as I took a bite of my tuna salad roll.

"I'm going to look for Jess myself and I'm going to find her. If anyone wants to help that would be . . . ." I paused. "Fantastic."

Sheila crunched on a chip.

I went on, "It's time to get to the bottom of all these rumors." May dropped her fork, and Sheila scurried to pick it up for her. As May stared at it skeptically, I forced myself to continue. "We need to listen and look for things we might not have noticed." I cleared my throat. "Like I just realized that Linda drives a red car."

May leaned across the table. "Excuse me?"

"It's just that everyone's talking about a red car," I said.

Sheila smirked. "Jesus, Caroline. They're looking for someone driving a red car to California, not Linda's car that is parked in the school lot right now. I thought you were supposed to be smart."

I glanced around the table. May had ratted me out about Tony. Sheila was awfully quick to put me down, and Billy looked like he was in a fog. Could I trust any of them? But I had to try. "I was just using it as an example. All I'm saying is we could start by asking kids we know if they've heard anything. We could listen in on conversations in the halls but pretend we're not listening. We might learn something important." Sheila tugged on her hoop earring. May nibbled on a carrot stick.

Billy started to speak, but May cut him off saying, "That sounds like a good idea, really. Of course we'll help. It's just so hard to know what to do." She looked up at the clock as if she was bored.

Sheila leaned close to her and said in a baby voice, "So a little birdy told me you and Billy are back together. Was Tweety right?" She glanced my way to make sure I heard.

May said, "We are."

I noticed she and Billy were holding hands. She had big hands for a girl, and long, fat fingers. They weren't delicate like mine. I tried not to look at him, but I couldn't help it. He'd kissed me. I'd thought he liked me.

In English, May asked to borrow a pencil and I gave her one, but I wouldn't give her the satisfaction of a smile. Then she asked to see the poem I'd written for the assignment due that day. I handed her "Death and the Buttercup" and watched as she bent over hers, scribbling furiously with *my pencil.*

"Last-minute inspiration," she said with a weak smile.

When Mr. Raymond said, "Who wants to read first?" there was a collective groan. He eyed May. "How about you, Miss Beckham?"

She dropped my pencil and made her way forward, one foot in front of the other in her charm school way. Her hands shook as she held up the sheet of paper, but before she could open her mouth he said, "One thing first. Can you answer a question?" She looked up.

Mr. Raymond smiled. "Is May short for anything? I find myself craving another syllable. Maybell. Maybelline?"

"No." She frowned, and he told her to go on.

"Thinner." Her lips sort of twitched as she read about wanting to be thin as a pin, as a grin, as the scar on the skin of a wrist that is slit, as a buttercup. I gasped as she added, "Before Death picks it." She'd not only stolen Billy. She'd stolen my poem. She stared at the class grimly, and hurried back to her seat.

Mr. Raymond stroked his chin. "Thank you, May. Any comments?" When no one replied, he turned to her. "What we have here is another poem in the fine tradition of poets who are half in love with easeful Death. Would that be correct, Miss Beckham?"

She sighed. "I guess."

I was relieved that the class ended before I had to read my poem. Mr. Raymond would probably have thought I'd copied her.

Lockers banged shut all around me as I grabbed my books. I was a fool for even trying this. I wasn't like Jess, meeting people at every turn, not caring if they didn't like her. I was too quiet. Kids rushed by without noticing me. They weren't going to talk to me. Billy wasn't going to be waiting at his locker for me, either. I slammed mine shut.

May came up behind me as I was heading outside. "I can't believe Mr. Raymond made me go first," she said breathlessly.

"Well, I can't believe you practically stole my poem," I said.

"That's not fair, Caroline. I just used it for inspiration."

I turned to her. "You know what's really unfair?" She raised an eyebrow. "That you didn't cover for me about Tony."

"It was your idea to go with him." She stepped back. "And you never told me to cover for you."

I sighed. "I suppose I never told you not to steal my poem, either."

She hunched her shoulders and looked down at the ground. "I don't even belong in that class."

Poor May, too tall, not thin enough.

"My brain is a like a dead frog," she said.

"Why don't you write a poem about that? It's a brilliant metaphor."

"Very funny, Caroline. You're so smart. You think of all these cool things so easily."

If I didn't know better I'd think she was jealous of me, but everything except poetry came easily to her. Girls like May always got what they wanted. And no one ever told her "no."

"Want to walk over to Billy's practice together?" She gave me her sweet smile.

I shrugged. "I'm not going today."

She frowned. "It's not good for you to sit in your room and write about death."

This was simply too much. "I have more important things to do than going to football practices. Like I told you at lunch, I have to find my sister."

She stared at me. "You're not mad at me about Billy, are you?"

Mad? I was livid. She hadn't even told me they were back together until now. "I thought you broke up with him. You said he was boring."

She paused, considering this. "I did, but things changed. Billy and I were together a long time. It's complicated with us. You can't expect me not to feel what I feel just because of what you feel. That wouldn't be fair, would it?" When I didn't answer she repeated, "Would it?" as if somehow I'd missed her ridiculous point.

It was no use arguing with her—she was always right. "No, it wouldn't be fair."

I started walking away.

"You can't make a person feel bad for something they didn't do," she called out after me. I pretended not to hear. She went in one direction toward where the playing fields were, and I went in the other. Billy's kiss wasn't that great, all teeth and tongues out of sync with each other. Nothing like the movies. And thinking about the orange soda taste in his mouth made me gag. May could have him.

I kicked a rock in the dust. So what if my friends couldn't be bothered to help me find Jess. I didn't need them. I'd talk to the person who'd been waiting for me after school almost every day this week, the person who knew my sister better than anyone, and who liked talking to me, though he wasn't talking to anyone else. The person who everyone told me *not* to talk to. I glanced across the street, disappointed to see that on today of all days he wasn't there. It figured. But as I was trudging home a car roared past, sending dust into my eyes. It banged a U-turn and fishtailed all over the road as it headed back my way. I squinted, my eyes stinging, and stopped dead in my tracks. No one else drove like that.

CHAPTER 12

Tony slowed to a stop beside me. Debbie sat next to him, wearing a white uniform, a silver snowflake pin gleaming on her collar. He leaned out the window and said, "Something wrong, Twinkle Toes?"

I sighed. If he only knew.

"Come on. Get in. I'll drive you home. It's too hot to walk." His eyes were swimming with sympathy. I climbed in the back. He went on, "I was driving Debbie to work when we saw you and I says, 'Isn't that Caroline?' And she says, 'Doesn't she look unhappy?' So I says, 'We better give her a ride.'" He grinned.

"You musta been dying out there. It's hotter than a firecracker lit at both ends," Debbie said.

Dying? I've been half in love with easeful Death, I thought. I glanced at the blue fuzzy dice dangling from the rearview mirror. There was a plastic figurine of Wile E. Coyote on the dash, and a gold bangle that didn't belong to Jess on the floor. I squirmed, the hot vinyl seat sticking to my thighs.

Tony said, "So tell me, why do you look so unhappy?"

My nerves raced. "It's nothing."

Tony shook his head. "You miss your sister?"

"Yeah, but . . . ."

"Something else?" He raised an eyebrow.

I stared into the black mirrors of my shoes. "I thought Billy liked me, but apparently he's back with May." It was stupid to be upset about such a small thing when Jess was missing, but it felt good to tell him.

Tony cast a quick glance at me. "Sorry to hear that darlin', but you can do better."

"Love stinks, and don't I know it," Debbie said. She turned to Tony. "You better step on it. My boss will kill me if I'm late."

"Don't worry, you'll make it." Tony pulled another screeching U-turn that made me nearly fall off the seat. "You don't mind if I drop Deb off first, do you? Can't have Snow White getting fired from the Frosty Queen." He turned and winked at me.

"That's okay." I gripped the edge of the seat.

She gazed into her compact mirror, more like the wicked queen than Snow White. Mirror on the wall, who's the fairest of them all? Definitely not Debbie Frank. She lit a cigarette, turned round, and casually blew smoke in my face. "So?" she asked.

Her chin was propped on the back of the seat, cigarette dangling from her fingertips. I could see her white lipstick and the little red velvet bow she always wore in her hair, like it lived there.

"I was talking to your lover-boy in school today," she said.

I caught my breath. "Billy?"

"He's in my math class. He's only a sophomore, so he must be real smart."

"Or you're real dumb," Tony said.

She glared at him and turned back to me. "I hardly know him, but he starts asking me about Jess—when I saw her last, if she was mad at Tony. Like he was a cop or something. Strange, huh?"

I cleared my throat. "That is strange."

"I thought so, too. I mean, why is *he* so interested?"

I tried to appear calm, though my heart was skittering. I couldn't believe Billy had actually started investigating. "I asked him to help me find Jess."

Tony smacked the steering wheel. "Just what I need, another private dick." He laughed. "Lately I can't even take a piss in private." My cheeks reddened. He flashed his blue eyes at me. "Sorry, forgot there was a lady present."

Debbie said, "She doesn't look like a lady to me. She looks like a little girl."

I frowned. "So what did you tell Billy?"

"Jesus," Debbie said. "What is this, the third degree?"

I swallowed hard. "I just want to find my sister."

Tony turned to her. "Cool it, Deb. She wants to find Jess as much as I do."

Debbie gave him an incredulous look. "No offense, Caroline, but your sister could be a real bitch. I'm surprised you miss her so much. You shoulda heard some of the things she said about you. You're probably the last thing on her mind while she's having a great time in California."

"I don't care. I just want to find her." I hated the way Debbie acted, as if she knew Jess better than I did.

Tony gave her a sidelong glance. "Just answer her, Deb."

"All right." She pouted. "I'll tell you exactly what I told Billy. The last time I saw Jess was at that party at the wash in the desert. She got mad at Tony for flirting with Edie." She glanced at Tony. "It's not like this is news to anyone."

"Who's Edie?" I asked.

"Just some girl," he said.

She glanced at him again. "She worships the ground Tony walks on."

I wondered if Edie could be what had gone wrong between Tony and Jess. This was all happening so fast, I'd forgotten to write it down. I pulled a notebook from my stack of books.

As I frantically scribbled notes, Debbie looked at me and said, "Are you kidding?"

"Caroline's a smart girl. Smart people take notes," Tony said.

Debbie took another puff of her cigarette. "All right, smarty, write this in your little book. Jess was out of control that night. I mean vicious, like she was on something." I winced. She continued, "I thought she was going to kill Tony when he tried to calm her down, but then this guy with a red car, who I've never seen before, said he'd drive her to California, and poof, she was gone." She snapped her fingers to illustrate.

Tony grunted. "She wasn't going to kill me."

"It's a figure of speech," Debbie said. "Smart people use figures of speech."

We were silent for a moment. Debbie was wrong. Jess wasn't vicious, but sometimes she did get out of control. At home, all of us except Dad knew that when this happened, yelling didn't do any good, and neither did reasoning. You had to let her go off until she came back. She always came back. I caught my breath. I couldn't let the conversation die just when I was learning something about what happened. "You sure you'd never seen the guy in the red car before?"

Debbie leaned so far over the back of the seat I worried she was going to come get me. "If I say I never seen him before, I never seen him before." She glared at me with her small mirror-mirror eyes. "I've already told the police all this. So you and lover-boy need to back off, okay?"

"Okay." I figured I'd asked enough for one day, and didn't say anything else as Tony drove like a maniac to get Debbie to work on time.

When we were almost at the ice cream place, Debbie turned around to me and said, "I'm sorry for saying those things about Jess." I sat up straighter. "I know you miss her. I do, too." She wiped some lipstick from the edge of her mouth. "And now that I think of it, I remember a little more about the guy who took her to California. He was tall, with light hair and acne scars on his face. He had some tattoos too; the kind guys get in prison. You might want to write that down in your little book."

I shuddered. It was completely unlike Jess to hang out with someone with bad skin.

Tony cast an anxious glance at me. "I pray to God he's taking care of your sister."

"Me too." Debbie watched as I wrote this down, Tony's words making me sick with worry. "Don't forget the part about the tattoo," she said. "You also might want to check out known criminals." She rolled her eyes. I bit my pencil.

We were in front of the Frosty Queen. After Debbie hopped out and disappeared inside, Tony said, "Don't mind her. Sometimes she can be a little frosty." He nodded toward the giant plastic head of a woman with sparkling snowflake eyes, looking down on us from the roof. I wiped my sweaty palms on my thighs and got in front.

He said, "Why don't we get an ice cream, and then I'll take you home." I nodded and he got out of the car, leaving it running, and called out, "Just drive it up the block if anyone gives you crap."

I gasped. I didn't know how to drive. I slumped down in the seat, remembering all those times when I was in back, Jess and Tony in the front, either lost in each other or fighting. Just a few weeks ago when Tony got us burgers, Jess's had mayonnaise though she hadn't asked for it. She said it was his fault, that he couldn't do anything right. He punched the steering wheel so hard there was blood on his knuckles. Then he stopped short, horns shrieking behind us, and told her to eat it or get out and walk. When she started to open the door, he yanked her back in. Her dark mood filled the car. Tony wouldn't even look at her. I knew better than to say a word. She sulked for the rest of the ride.

I glanced down the street, dreading that someone would pull up behind me and make me move the car. I was relieved when Tony finally returned, an ice cream in each hand. He passed me a soft-serve vanilla. "Your favorite, right?"

"How'd you know that?"

"I know everything about you."

I remembered that when we came here with Jess, I always got vanilla. "Vanilla for the girl who's afraid of her own shadow," Jess had said once, and I'd been angry that she thought she understood me, and more angry that it was true. Now I swirled my tongue around my ice cream, but not fast enough to prevent a drip from running down my hand.

Tony licked his chocolate cone rapidly around and around. As the scoop got smaller, I realized I was staring at his tongue. For a moment it was just the two of us sitting in the hot car, licking, like two cats with bowls of milk. When Tony was through, he tossed the tip of his sugar cone out the window, started to back up, and stopped.

"Caroline, I gotta tell you." I tensed. "Edie doesn't mean anything to me. I tried to explain that to Jess, but she didn't get it. Anytime a girl would look at me she'd flip out, but I put up with it because I didn't want to lose her." He gave me a quick glance. His downward-tilting eyes, dark lashes, and small mouth reminded me of a sad French clown doll, called a Pierrot, I'd gotten for Christmas years ago.

I wanted to ask him more, but being so close to him made my words dry up. I opened my notebook, doodled a flower, and forced myself to say, "Do you have any idea who the blond man who drove Jess could have been?"

"I told you I didn't know." He pulled out onto Speedway.

I sighed. "Is there anything else you remember about that night I should know?"

"You think I'm just gonna tell you everything?"

I blushed. "No, but you want to find Jess. I know you do."

"I do, but I've got to trust you first."

I looked out the window. "You can trust me."

On the radio someone sang about being oh so lonely. He reached over and touched my hand. "I'll tell you the real reason she was mad at me. How about that?"

"Okay." I slid my hand out from under his.

"We didn't go to the drive-in that night." I caught my breath as he went on, "Jess had her heart set on going dancing." He gave me a sad glance. The memory must have been difficult for him. "I told her I didn't want to go 'cause there was a party in the desert. She didn't want to hear that. You know how she is?"

I nodded.

Tony sighed. "When we got to the party and she saw Edie, Jess decided she was the reason I wouldn't go dancing. She said a few things she shouldn't have said." He glanced my way. "Your sister has a knack for saying things that set people off." His hands tightened around the steering wheel. "And I said a few things I shouldn't have said, too. Then she left with that guy. I'm real sorry. So there it is. Hope it helps."

I wanted to write it down, but it seemed wrong at a moment like this. "It does," I said quietly.

He checked his side mirror. "Good, 'cause now I have a question for you."

I stiffened.

"She was supposed to bring you with her that night, right?" I nodded and he added, "Why do you think she didn't?"

"All she said was something important was going on, something she couldn't talk about."

He scratched his head. "Strange. Don't know what she could have been referring to. Did she mention going dancing?"

"No."

"You sure?" He turned and stared at me so hard it made me flinch. Out of the corner of my eye I saw a car heading directly for us and screamed. He grabbed the wheel with both hands and veered away, sending us skidding into some scrub. Without even blinking, he brought the car back on the road.

"Jesus H. Christ," he said. "Some people really don't know how to drive."

"That was a close call," I said. My whole body was shaking.

"No, it wasn't." He turned to me for a second. "I don't have close calls." He roared past the truck in front of us.

I worried that he was mad at me, but he said, "I've been trying to come up with a plan for finding Jess, like I said I would. I think sharing what we know about her is the way to begin."

"I agree. That whole night was strange. I've tried over and over, but I can't figure it out."

"And I can't, either." He paused. "But I bet we can figure it out together. That's what you want, right?"

"Yes." It was what I had to say, but I couldn't believe I'd said it.

"Great. Then we're a team." A team. I smiled. We were almost at my house. Tony pulled up to the curb. We sat there a moment in silence.

"Remember when I told you that you were as pretty as May?" he finally said. "The only thing she has over you is her hair." He leaned close. "I'm gonna let you in on a little secret. If you dye yours blonde, you'll get Billy back." He pushed a strand out of my face.

I looked up at him. "My mom would kill me if I dyed my hair."

"Did she kill Jess when she dyed her hair?" I shook my head. "So why should you be any different?"

"She lets Jess do all kinds of things she won't let me do."

He put his hand on mine. "Maybe it's time to change that." His palm was rough and warm. He went on, "I can dye it for you, if you want. If you don't like the way it looks, I'll dye it back. What do you say?"

"I don't know." Out the window, the green fronds of the palm trees were raised as if in a prayer to the sky. "Can you dye it Ivory Chiffon?"

He gave my hand a squeeze. "Of course. I'll pick you up tomorrow and take you to my house and do it there. I know how. I do it for all the beautiful girls." I shifted in my seat, still unsure. "Come on, it will make me happy." He turned my face to his. "And maybe I'll have more to tell you about your sister."

"Okay." I tried to ignore the nervous fluttering in my chest.

CHAPTER 13

Tony was waiting for me after school the next day. He'd even bought a bottle of hair dye.

"I have a Spanish test tomorrow, so I can't stay too long," I warned him as I settled myself on the seat.

"Don't worry, you won't fail your test." As he put his arm on the seat behind me, I smelled his lime cologne.

A few minutes later we pulled up in front of his parents' ranch-style house. On the way to the small guesthouse in back, we passed a pool with blue-green water as still as Jell-O. I almost tripped on a beer bottle someone had left on the yellow and black Mexican tiles that bordered it. I wondered if it was from one of Tony's parties.

"Watch it, hon." He cupped my elbow, his touch so soft it startled me.

I gulped. The windows of the guesthouse were painted black. I'd never been this close to it before. Jess preferred it when Tony took her to the movies or out to eat on Speedway. She said she wasn't content to hang out in his house, like the other girls who liked him. He understood that to win a girl like her, a girl who was a cut above, he couldn't treat her like them.

Tony flashed me a smile. "I like my privacy."

The purple beaded curtain rattled as he pushed it aside and led me into a big room with a kitchen at one end. It was even hotter in there than outside, the ceiling fan doing little good. Two girls were seated on a velvet couch, watching a television with a silk scarf dangling from one of the rabbit ears. A rug patterned with brown, yellow, and black lay on the red tiled floor. A stick of incense burning in a small brass Buddha filled the air with the scent of spice. Magazines and papers were scattered everywhere, but it was a beautiful kind of mess, so different from my boring, neatly arranged house.

One of the girls smiled at me. I gasped. She had pure white hair.

Tony went over to the small kitchen at other end of the room and talked to a tall guy wearing jeans and cowboy boots standing by the fridge. I stood in front of the fireplace, admiring a framed black-and-white photo of the desert on the mantel. The sand was rippled like water, bare except for some silver driftwood that was as smooth as bone. Someone had written, "My witness is the empty sky" on a cloud.

Next to the photo was a bottle of Johnnie Walker Black, the same kind of scotch my uncle Fred gave Dad for Christmas every year. I picked it up gingerly. A cigarette butt was floating in the half inch of liquid at the bottom. My fingers trembled at the thought that maybe this was the same bottle Jess had stuffed in her purse before she climbed out the window.

"Want some?"

I almost dropped the bottle. Tony had crept up behind me.

"No." I put it back down.

"Have a seat." He pointed toward a maroon easy chair. "Moose and I are going out by the pool to talk business. You girls get to know each other."

I looked up at the big guy from the kitchen standing next to him. His head practically touched the ceiling fan and he had wide-set, bulging eyes, and straight brown hair that fell below his ears. He looked like a giant with a friendly smile.

"Business?" I said after they went outside.

The girl with the white hair pushed away her shaggy bangs, revealing large, brown eyes. "He sells pot."

My mouth fell open.

She smiled. "So, how do ya know Tony?"

I ran my finger around a cigarette burn on the arm of the chair. "I'm Caroline, Jess's sister." I waited for the inevitable silence then pity.

"I'm Edie." I caught my breath. So this was the girl Jess was so angry about. Her white hair was long and stringy, and she was skinny, no figure at all. She didn't seem any older than I was. Her face was pretty except for a slightly bent nose and a faint scar by her mouth. She said, "I used to see Jess around here sometimes."

The other girl turned to me. Her hair was as long as Edie's but it was brown and curly. Silver earrings dangled from her ears. "You look like her, but different. You don't have the attitude."

Edie shot her a glance. "Cool it, Lizzie. You're talking about her sister."

"That's okay. I know what Jess is like." I fidgeted with the buckle of the rawhide belt I'd worn with my favorite jean skirt.

There was a loud splash. Edie looked at Lizzie and then said, "They must be swimming."

"Saints be praised." Lizzie twirled a curl around her finger. I raised my eyebrows.

Edie turned to me. "No one has used the pool since that party when your sister disappeared."

A cold finger touched my heart. "Why not?"

Edie frowned. "Tony told us not to use it even if it's like a thousand degrees out." Her eyes shone as she added, "He has a thing about water. He respects its power 'cause he almost drowned. He died, you know, and then he came back to life."

I nodded.

Lizzie rolled her eyes. "Like Lazarus."

Edie folded her arms across her chest. "It's true."

Lizzie frowned. "Along with UFOs and the Easter Bunny." She glanced at me. "If you're smart, you won't believe a word she says. Tony's just superstitious and doesn't want anyone to swim in his precious pool . . . ." She paused. "Until Jess comes back." She looked at me intently. "But something must have changed."

I froze. Could he be swimming because we really were going to find her, because we were a team now? I leaned forward. "Did you see Jess the night she disappeared?"

Edie and Lizzie looked at each other. Edie said, "I was at that party in the desert." She continued in a hushed voice, "Jess picked a fight with Tony there. She was real mad." She glanced around. "I probably shouldn't say this, but she was mad 'cause of me. Tony gave me a ring. I'll show you if you want."

I felt like the wind had been knocked out of me. Tony had said Edie meant nothing to him. "Okay."

While she was off looking for the ring, Lizzie said, "Edie makes a big deal out of everything, but she's not the first girl Tony has given a ring to. He probably gave one to Jess, right?"

"Right," I said, though I had no idea.

"I'm probably the only girl on the planet Tony hasn't given a ring to, and you, of course."

"Of course."

Though Tony had never given her one, Lizzie had a silver ring on every finger. She pushed her long hair from her face. "I'd smoked a couple of joints the night of that party, so everything is like in a haze, but I do remember how mad your sister was. I think she was pissed 'cause of Edie. She and Tony really went at it, those two."

I hugged my knees, trying to stay calm.

Lizzie went on, "I couldn't believe the things coming out of your sister's mouth that night. She was talking so fast, no one could get a word in. It was like she was on something. I'd never seen her so nervous."

"What was she talking about?" I chewed on a nail. Jess wasn't the nervous type, but she'd been upset about something before she left that night.

"She might have called Tony a lying bastard. But I don't remember much else." She shrugged.

"Did you see her leave in a red car?" My throat was so dry I coughed.

"Red car?" Lizzie looked puzzled. "She might have left with Tony and some of his friends, but I didn't actually *see* her go anywhere. I was too busy seeing little green Martians and conversing with the flowers, if you know what I mean."

I had no idea what she meant. I read about drugs, but I'd never known anyone who took them. If Jess had, she'd never told me. I leaned closer to Lizzie. "Debbie said she left with a blond guy in a red car."

She sighed. "She could have. I was so stoned; I was kind of on another planet." She smiled.

Edie walked in holding a small white velvet box. She opened it, revealing a gold ring with a glittering green stone in it. "It's real." She beamed at me.

Lizzie smirked. "Real. What does that mean? Everything is real, isn't it?"

Edie rolled her eyes. "Lizzie, the philosopher." She placed the ring on my palm. "It's a real emerald, my favorite."

"Really?" It looked about as genuine as the bracelet from the Emerald City that Dad had given Mom, but I told her it was pretty.

"Real pretty glass," Lizzie said.

Edie glared at her. "Tony saved up his money for months for this." She put it back in the white box. "I don't dare wear it 'cause

I'll lose it. I lose everything." She smiled, showing small pointy incisors that looked like fangs.

She put the box on the messy coffee table where I was pretty sure it would get lost and said, "Jess was livid when she heard about my ring." Lizzie looked up and smirked again. Edie said, "She *was* mad about it. She even threatened Tony."

"What do you mean?" I asked.

She spoke in a voice barely above a whisper. "She said if he didn't dump me she was going to tell something about him he didn't want anyone to know."

I stepped closer. Could this be the thing that Jess hadn't wanted to talk to me about?

Lizzie raised her eyebrows. "I don't remember Jess saying that." She turned to me. "Edie's a liar. Pathological. She can't help herself."

With her skinny arms and big eyes, she didn't look like a pathological anything. As she started to say something else, the door opened and Tony came in with Moose.

Tony's jeans were soaked and he'd taken his shirt off. Though I tried not to look, I couldn't take my eyes off his thickly muscled arms, pale and glistening, his dark nipples, the thin line of hair going down the middle of his stomach. Moose put a six-pack on the table, sat down between Edie and Lizzie, draped an arm around each one, and said, "How're my ladies today?"

Edie wriggled away. "You're wet."

Moose wrapped his arms around her waist. "Why don't you come skinny-dipping with me, and then we'll both be wet."

"Let me go." She shook him off, and reached for a beer. "You want some?"

I told her no.

"You don't have to share mine. You can have your own." She smiled, showing those incisors again.

Moose handed me one. Tony winked at me. "Caroline's too young to drink."

"Caroline? Jess's little sister?" Moose looked startled.

Tony smiled. "I'm gonna dye her hair blonde."

Moose shook his head. "Tony's a regular hairdresser."

Tony leaned down and whispered in my ear, "Don't listen to anything Moose says. His brain is fried. He's taken too many artificial substances, if you catch my drift." Edie giggled and Tony said, "Come on, I need your help. Take Caroline to the bathroom while I put on some dry clothes."

She glanced at Lizzie. "You want to help, too?"

"God, no." She said to Tony, "When you're done, can you give me a ride home?"

"Sure thing, sugarplum." He grinned. "Jesus, everybody wants me today."

Edie, pathological liar, I thought as I followed her into a small bathroom with yellow and white tiles and a round shag rug that probably used to be yellow.

"Tony's an expert at dyeing hair," she said. "He likes his girls to look a certain way. He did mine." She draped a towel on my shoulders. Her hair was white as snow, except for the dark roots at the part. With her wide brown eyes, she looked like a creature from a fairy tale. Though it was wrong, the thought of being one of "his girls" gave me a thrill.

Tony came in a moment later. He told me to sit down on the toilet, went over to the small window on the opposite wall, and stared out. I could see the dusty sole of one of his boots as he tapped his toe on the tile, the edge of his wallet sticking out from the curve of his back pocket. I was so close to him I could smell his sweat mixed with cologne. Soon I'd be a blonde. I knew it shouldn't scare me, but it did.

"Don't worry." He pivoted around and put a bottle of hair dye down on the edge of the sink. "You don't have to go as extreme as Edie did."

"I don't like to do nothing halfway." She smiled.

I started to get up, wishing to go home, but Tony put his hand on my shoulder. "Edie is a Marilyn Monroe type, but I see you as more the Jane Asher type." He ran his finger along my cheekbone. I shivered. It was so strange. Jess had said the same thing. I sat back down.

"Relax. I got you Ivory Chiffon, just like you asked for." Tony put on some rubber gloves.

"Jane Asher isn't a blonde," Edie said.

"But she'd look better as one." Tony winked at me, and squirted the dye onto my hair and massaged it in. His touch was strong but soothing as he pressed his fingers into my scalp. The stuff smelled noxious. I squeezed my eyes shut. Some dye ran down my forehead and I started to wipe it away, but Tony said, "Don't move."

When he was through, Edie wrapped my hair up in the towel. Tony stepped back and looked at me. "Now all you gotta do is wait," he said. He pulled off the rubber gloves and dropped them in the sink.

CHAPTER 14

"You still need that ride?" Tony said to Lizzie, when we were back in the living room. She nodded. He placed his hands on my shoulders. "I'll be back soon. Edie will keep you company." He glanced at her. "You girls can clean this place up while we're gone."

"You're going to be so pretty when your hair is done," she said when they'd left.

"I hope so."

"This place is such a mess." She began clearing things off the coffee table, including some *Playboy* magazines, like the ones Dad kept under his bed. I picked up an overflowing ashtray and followed her to the kitchen area. She filled the sink up with soapy water and put in some egg-encrusted dishes from the counter.

"I'll wash. You dry," she said. "Tony's mom usually does this for him, but I like to help." I smiled. I'd heard the stories about how Tony's mom cleaned and sometimes made drinks for his parties.

As Edie washed the dishes with surprising efficiency, she said, "Tony's taking Lizzie to pick up her baby sister. Lizzie watches her at night when her mom's at work." She paused. "Tony lets Lizzie stay over with the baby whenever she wants to. He even buys diapers and formula. He loves helping people." She gazed up at the fly-filled light fixture. I was surprised Jess hadn't mentioned any of this.

She passed me a dish to dry. "Can you keep a secret?"

I slid the cloth over the dish, thinking, here it comes, my reason for being here. "Yes."

Her brown eyes widened. "It isn't really Lizzie's little sister."

"No?"

"No." Her eyes grew even wider. "It's her baby, and she doesn't even know who the dad is."

"How old is she?"

Edie shook her head. "Sixteen. She looks older, doesn't she? She's so lucky to have Tony. If he didn't drive her places and let her hang out here, she'd be stuck at home all the time."

"She doesn't go to school?"

"Lizzie had to drop out, but it's no big deal. They don't teach you anything worth much in school. I dropped out, too. Just because I wanted to." She looked proud of this.

"How old are you?"

"Fifteen."

"I'm fifteen, too," I said. "I hate high school."

"You should drop out. Then we could hang out all the time."

I shook my head. Much as I hated it, I couldn't imagine not going. You had to go to high school. "I'd like to, but my mom would kill me."

"Promise me you'll think on it," Edie said. "My mom says as long as I don't hit her up for money, I can do what I want. And since Tony and I are going be married, it doesn't matter so much if I'm in school."

"Married?" I almost dropped the plate I was holding.

She stared at me as if I were an idiot. "He gave me a ring."

"Aren't you a little young to get married?" Tony was going to marry Jess, and now he was going to marry Edie? This didn't make sense.

She frowned. "You and your bourgeois attitude. Tony says when it comes to love, there are no rules. There's only feelings."

My sister would have been furious if she'd found this out. "But what about Jess? She's Tony's girlfriend, you know."

Edie bit her lower lip. "Look, I know she's your sister and all, but I mean, where is she? You can't expect Tony to wait around for someone who just up and disappears."

She had a point. It would be just like Jess to take off in a huff and expect the whole world to stop and wait while she was gone.

Outside the small window above the sink, a black and yellow bird landed on a wooden fence. As it opened and closed its beautiful wings, I felt a catch in my throat. Had Jess ever seen a bird like that here? Had she thought it was beautiful? Did she even notice?

"I suppose," I said. Edie handed me a glass to dry.

As I reached into it with the dishcloth, she touched my shoulder. "The day of that party, Jess wouldn't stop calling Tony. She drove him crazy." She reached into the soapy water. "He wanted to break up with her, but he didn't want to hurt her feelings." She paused. "If I had anything to do with her running away, I'm sorry."

"It's okay." I stared at the water-splattered floor, wishing Jess had told me more about what was going on. If she had, I could have talked her out of leaving.

Edie wiped her wet hands on her jeans. "I want to marry Tony more than anything, but if Jess comes back and Tony wants her and she wants him, I can deal with that. No point in not going with the flow. Everything comes around sooner or later."

She twisted the leather bracelet on her wrist. "Do you believe in other lives?" Before I could answer she said, "I do. Tony says no one dies. They just step out of one body and into another. He learned that when he almost drowned." She looked out the window. The bird spread its black and gold wings and flew away.

"I hope that's true," I said. "But that would mean there are no ghosts." I eyed her, thinking of the rumors May had mentioned.

She gave me a shove. "There are ghosts. Sometimes spirits get trapped in this place between lives called the bardo. You can read all about it in *The Tibetan Book of the Dead*." She hesitated. "You can summon spirits, but you gotta be real careful if you summon a bad one."

She was making my head spin. "So have you summoned a spirit?"

She smiled. "No, of course not."

I put the dishcloth down. I had to ask her one more thing. "You didn't see the blond guy who was driving the red car, did you?"

For a moment she looked like she didn't know what I was talking about. Then she said, "Now that I think of it, maybe I did. He was the real handsome type Jess would like."

"Handsome? Debbie said he looked like he just got out of prison."

She bit her lower lip. "There are handsome guys in prison. But maybe he wasn't. I didn't look that close." I wondered if Lizzie was right and Edie really was a liar. Debbie said he was a criminal with bad skin. Edie said he was handsome. Someone was lying.

"It's strange the way Debbie always hangs around Tony, though she's nothing to him." Edie wrinkled her nose. "She reminds me of a dead fish, cold and creepy."

"Especially with her white lipstick," I said.

She smiled, stood behind me and unwrapped the towel from my head. "Let me rinse your hair out, and then we'll sit out in the sun until it's dry."

As we sat on lounge chairs beside the pool, I shut my eyes and let the heat press down on me. I must have fallen asleep, because the next thing I knew Edie was shaking me, saying, "Come on, you have to see yourself. You look great."

When we went back inside, I stood on my tiptoes to see myself in the mirror over the mantel. My hair was a golden blonde. I didn't look like May, or Jane Asher. I didn't even look like me.

"Do you like it?" she said.

I looked more closely. At least it wasn't as light as Edie's. "I guess."

Edie pressed her face next to mine in the mirror and was saying, "We're like twins," when Tony and Moose came back.

Edie grinned at them. "What do you think?"

Tony stared at me, a look on his face as if he'd seen a ghost. I touched my hair. Was something wrong? He came over and stood so close behind me I could feel his warm breath on my neck. He lifted my hair and let it fall. "Lovely," he said. He turned my face toward him. "Like you." He studied me intently, his eyes like a blue drink, two parts sadness, one part loneliness. It was hard to turn away.

"You really like it?" I said.

"I do." He took my hand. I glanced at Edie, hoping she wasn't jealous.

Moose was gawking at me, his mouth open, as if he couldn't believe what he saw. He started to say, "She looks just like . . . " when Tony put his finger to his lips, and he stopped.

Nervous, I stepped away and pointed to the photo on the mantel. "'My witness is the empty sky.' What does that mean?"

"You'll have to ask Jack Kerouac." Tony smiled. "He wrote that book *On the Road*. I'm a fan of his. He's a free thinker, like me."

"I've heard of him. Was Jess a fan?" I asked.

He looked at me sadly. "She wasn't like you. She never paid attention to anything but what she wanted." I nodded. The quietness in the room crept up around us.

"I'm so hungry I could eat a moose." Moose grinned.

"Come on." Edie led me over to the fridge. "They have to be fed." She pulled out a package of hot dogs, put a pot of water on the stove, and dumped them in. Then she stood on a chair and began rummaging in the cabinets above the sink. "I feel like baking a cake for the party tonight."

"Party?" I asked.

"It's always a party at Tony's." Her smiled faded, both of us remembering that other party. I thought again of what Edie had said about Jess threatening to reveal something about Tony. It didn't make sense. Jess wouldn't tell on Tony or anyone. But she had said something important was going on, something she couldn't talk about.

The room filled with the smell of boiled hot dogs, their pink skins splitting as they bounced around in the pot. My stomach lurched. I glanced at my watch. It was five o'clock. If I didn't make it home for dinner tonight, especially with my hair dyed blonde, there was no telling how much trouble I'd be in.

"I'm sorry," I said to Edie. "But I've got to go home now."

"I'll give you a ride," Tony said.

She pouted. "But Caroline didn't even have her hot dog."

I told her maybe next time.

As we walked by the pool, I tried to catch a glimpse of myself, but it was full of cloudy green shadows.

When we got in the car, the way Tony stared at me, as if I was someone else, someone I couldn't possibly be, made me nervous. I slid over close to the door. He lit a cigarette, checked himself out in the rearview mirror, and started the car up, the cigarette hanging out of his mouth as he backed out of the driveway.

This afternoon had left me with more questions than answers. They were all swirling around in my head, and with Tony sitting next to me, I was afraid to ask anything. He was the most important person to talk to, but also the hardest. But there was one question I had to ask. I took a deep breath, trying to be brave for my sister.

"Tony." I struggled to clear my throat. "Did you and Jess fight about anything other than Edie?"

He fiddled with the radio. "Why? Did Edie tell you something?" He settled on a song called "I Know a Place" about a place where your worries can't find you. He glanced at me. "Because if she did, I hope you realize she's a liar."

"I've heard that."

He tapped his hand on the steering wheel to the beat of the music. "You can't trust a word that comes out of her mouth. I tried to explain that to Jess, but she wouldn't listen."

I leaned my head against the seat, wishing that the big hopeful song would lift my worries from me. "I love this song," I said.

He cast a quick glance my way. "Me too."

Before I knew it, we were about a block from my house. He pulled up to the curb. "Better get out here so Mom and Dad don't see me." His pushed my hair behind my ear and said, "I like you as a blonde."

"Really?"

He nodded. "But you know what the best thing is?" I looked up. "You're not sad anymore."

"You mean about Billy?"

"No. You know what I mean."

I did. All these weeks, sadness had seeped into everything I'd done. But now, for the moment at least, it wasn't there. I was amazed that Tony knew this. It was like he could see straight into my heart. No one had ever done that before. "I've been thinking," he went on. He turned the radio down. "Remember how you told me Jess said something was going on that she couldn't talk about?" I nodded. "Did she say anything else strange that night that might help us figure out what she was referring to?"

"There is one thing."

He raised his eyes.

"As she climbed out the window, she said, 'Would you?'"

"Would you?"

"She didn't finish the question."

"You sure that's all she said?" He sounded a little mad. I could almost feel the roughness of his beard beneath his fingers as he scratched his chin. "And you didn't talk about anything else that night?"

I looked down at the dirty floor mat. "I asked her about Arnie."

"That dude from California?"

"I thought maybe she was going to break up with you," I said softly.

"Honey." He touched my cheek. "Jess wasn't going to break up with me."

I sat stone still with his hand on my cheek. It was so close and hot in the car, I felt like I couldn't breathe. He was half facing me, his legs slightly parted. He slid his hand down my cheek and then lightly touched the tip of my nose. "Caroline," he said.

"What," I almost shouted.

"Caroline," he repeated. He pulled me close and then he was kissing me. It wasn't like with Billy. His lips were soft, his hand tight against the small of my back. Feelings rose up from deep inside me, like I was on fire and sad and weeping at the same time. When he let me go, I turned away. He was Jess's boyfriend. How could I have kissed him?

He smoothed my hair. "I shouldn't have done that."

"It's okay," I said in a voice that was almost not a voice. It was as if he'd heard my thoughts. He took my hand and we sat there in the hot car for a timeless time, while on the radio a song that sounded far away played over and over.

He touched me softly under the chin. His fingers tickled. "Try to remember more. I will, too, and we'll talk about it next time. If we work together, we'll find Jess. I promise you."

"Okay," I said, thinking, together?

I fiddled with a pearl button on my blouse. When I was younger, my mom told me that she liked pearls because they capture the sea and moon in a little ball. It was so strange for her to say something like this that I never forgot it. Now I looked down at the innocent little button on my shirt and thought, I have the sea and moon right here before my eyes. I thought of what Edie said about just going with the flow. All this time I'd been trying so hard and nothing worked out for me, but now it was like everything was moving and opening up all at once. Of course we'd find Jess—together. I could almost see her, lovely and tiny, seated on the petal of giant flower.

As I opened the car door, Tony stroked my arm. "I can't get over your hair. It's like you're her." He gathered it up in a ponytail, then let it fall.

"I know a place," he said, just like in the song, "in California where the kids go sometimes. There are lots of people there and those people know other people. I bet she's there."

CHAPTER 15

I hurried into the kitchen. As I sat down at the table, Mom and Dad looked up at me. The room became too quiet. I wondered if I was in trouble.

Dad put down his fork. "You look different."

"She dyed her hair, Jack," Mom said.

He took a sip of his scotch. "For a minute I thought you were . . . ."

Mom stiffened.

"Someone else," he said.

As she slid a plate in front of me, she knocked my glass over and rushed to pick it up. "Thank God it didn't break," she said. "That was one of my good ones."

We were having sweet-and-sour chicken with pineapple chunks and a cherry on top, one of my favorite dinners. As I raised my fork to my lips, the memory of Tony's kiss, sweeter than the pineapple, went through me. Dad was right about one thing. I was different. Maybe I didn't look all that different, but the feeling from being in the car with Tony was still inside me. It was like someone had turned on a light in a dark room. The shine of the brass chandelier, the delicate wheat pattern on the plates, Mom's pearly moonbeam nail polish, Dad's reddish hair threaded with gray, the sunburn across the bridge of Dicky's nose—all these things competed for my attention. Jess couldn't stay lost in a world as full of bright and beautiful things as this one.

Mom fixed her steely gaze on me. "Did it ever occur to you to ask me before dyeing your hair?"

I looked down at my plate. "I didn't think you'd mind. May helped me. My hair's the same color as hers now. We're like twins."

As I ate a cherry, I thought of asking May to cover for me, but there wasn't much point in that. I couldn't trust her. I hoped Mom wouldn't talk to Betty about it. She gave Dad an agonized glance. He squeezed her hand. All I'd done was dye my hair. They were acting like the world was ending.

"You don't look anything like May," Mom said.

"I think you look nice." Dad smiled at me.

"Nice?" Mom folded her napkin by her plate. "You think it's nice that every time I look at her now, I'll think of Jess?" Her eyes gleamed with tears as she stood up.

"Frances." He reached for her, but she walked right past him and left the room.

I turned to Dad. "I wasn't trying to look like Jess."

"I know, kitten." He lowered his eyes. "This has been hard on your mother." I nodded. Lately the slightest thing could set her off, and she'd been having attacks of "nerves" and headaches and spending hours in her room. Dad finished the rest of his scotch and went over to the kitchen counter to pour himself another. He raised his drink to his lips, his bloodshot eyes not seeing me as he looked out over the rim of his glass. My appetite was gone. I hadn't meant to hurt either of them by looking like Jess. I wanted so much to tell them how Tony and I were going to find her, but I couldn't do that. If they found out, they'd never let me out of their sight.

In a few minutes Mom came back in and we finished our dinner. Dad took Dicky out to the backyard to look at the stars, but I stayed and helped her clean up. When we were through, she sat down at the kitchen table, took a few puffs of her cigarette, and then stubbed it out. "Go on outside with your dad," she said.

As I clicked the sliding glass door shut, I turned to see her with her face in her hands, sobbing.

Dad was in the middle of the yard with Dicky. I went over to them and looked up at the faint stars dotting the darkness. Dad used to take Jess and me outside to stargaze when we were younger. Sometimes he even used his telescope. Much as I loved it, I was always a little disappointed at how small and far away everything was.

He wrapped his arms around Dicky's waist now and said, "Hey bud, did you know it would take more than a lifetime to count all the stars?" More than a lifetime, I thought. If what Edie said was true and we jumped from one life into the next, were our lives as numerous as the stars, as uncountable? A desert wind chilled the grass beneath my feet. I reminded myself that the stars were giants, even though they looked like bitter little bits of brightness from here. And lives were beyond measuring.

Dicky looked up with Dad. "One, two, three, five, eleven."

"Just keep counting," Dad said, his eyes on the heavens as he counted along with him.

As Dad went on and on in a singsong voice, I wanted to shout, "Don't you know Mom is crying in there? Stop counting. Stop. Stop. Do something!" But I said nothing, for fear of losing the fragile hope inside me. It was like a glass of milk filled to the brim; the slightest misstep and it would spill.

I left the two of them standing there, and headed inside. Mom had gotten up from the table and was furiously scrubbing the counter even though it was already pretty clean. She didn't turn around as I walked by, but I didn't care. Maybe my whole family was falling apart, but I wasn't going to. Dad was drinking and counting, and Mom was sobbing and scrubbing, but I was going to find my sister.

As I sat on my bed, I picked up my notebook and wrote down what I'd learned so far. Tony said he and Jess fought about dancing. Edie said they fought about her. Tony said Edie was nothing to him. Edie said they were getting married. Debbie said the man in the red car looked like a criminal. Edie said he was handsome. Lizzie hadn't even seen the red car. Edie said that Jess threatened to reveal something Tony didn't want anyone to know. Lizzie said Edie was a liar. Tony said Edie was a liar, too. My head was reeling with all of this. Someone had to be lying. Tony might even be lying, but when I was with him, I felt closer to the truth.

I went over to the mirror and looked at my hair. It made my eyes appear darker, more mysterious, like real tigers' eyes. I was glad I'd dyed it. As I pulled it back I thought of Tony looking at me as if I was Jess, but also as if I was someone new who he wanted to get to know. I touched my lips. The tingle from his kiss was still there.

That night as I was drifting off to sleep, a warm, soft feeling started at the pit of my stomach and rose up all the way through me. It was sad and sweet at the same time. In the darkness behind my shut lids I saw Tony like a strange, unearthly cartoon, his hair black as coal, the loneliness in his blue eyes like the whispering of the sea when it kisses the sand.

I wasn't hallucinating. I wasn't going crazy. I saw him in the place between lives.

On Friday I ran into Billy in the hall. He was excited about having talked to Debbie about the guy in the red car. When I told him that Debbie told me the same thing when Tony gave me a ride home, he said, "I can't believe you got in a car with that guy. We're a team. Let me handle that part, Galvin."

"A team?" I said.

"Yeah. Detectives always work in teams." There was a goofy grin on his infinitely freckled face. "Nice hair, Caroline," he said.

"Glad you like it." I pushed a strand behind my ear. For a detective, Billy had been pretty clueless about how I felt. "I'm sorry, but I think we can help each other more by working separately. I'll get Tony to trust me so he'll talk to me, and you can work undercover and find out stuff from his friends."

He pulled me over to a locker out of the rushing crowd of kids. "Caroline, I already went undercover."

I clutched my books to my chest. "Did you find anything out?"

"I tried to listen in while Debbie was talking to some kids, but she told me to get lost."

I smiled. "That sounds like her. She already told you everything she's going to tell you."

He stared at his long sneakered feet. "But something she said about the red car doesn't feel right to me."

"Why?" I felt a flicker of fear.

He scratched his head. "Just a hunch, I guess."

"Debbie told me the guy in the red car was blond with bad skin." I paused. "He might be a criminal."

"Do you think that's true?"

"I don't know. I really can't see Jess driving across the country with someone like that, but why would Debbie lie?"

"Because she's a liar?" Billy looked at me. "Her story changes every time she opens her mouth. She told you he had blond hair. She told me she didn't remember anything about him, and if I asked any more she'd have Tony take care of me." He clenched his fist. "He better not try anything with me."

"Debbie didn't mean it. She likes to act tough." I couldn't believe I was defending Debbie Frank.

Billy leaned over me, his hand pressed against the wall. "But why would she tell me one thing and you another?"

"Maybe she trusts me more," I said without actually believing it. All the different stories I'd heard made me uneasy.

He shook his head. "It doesn't add up."

The crowd in the corridor was thinning out. The bell for the next class rang. "I've got to go," I said.

He put his hand on my arm. "Wait. There's something else." He bit his lip. "I *did* see something that night."

"What?" I said.

He took a deep breath like this was hard to tell me. "Remember how I said I was riding my bike home from the party and I wiped out? That isn't exactly what happened."

I frowned. "What did happen?"

"A car sped by and came so close it clipped me, and I went flying into a ditch." He tugged on his shirt collar. "Caroline, there was a girl leaning out the window of the car screaming. Someone pulled her back in. It wasn't a red car. It was Tony's car, and she had blonde hair. I'm worried it might have been Jess."

All the air rushed out of me. "Do you really think so?"

"It was dark. I was drunk." He stared at me grimly. "I didn't think so at first, but now all this red car stuff is making me wonder. I don't know."

I felt my hope draining away. He moved closer and placed his arm around me. "That can't be true," I said.

"It might not have been her. The car was going so fast I didn't get a good look." He pushed my hair off my shoulder. "I didn't mean to upset you. I just wanted to help." My breath was coming in quick gasps. "You'll be all right," he said softly. A couple of weeks ago I would have longed for this moment, but now all I wanted was for it never to have happened.

"Oh, God." I shoved him away. "Why didn't you tell anyone about this until now?"

"My dad would beat the crap out of me if he found out I was at a party in the desert." He snuck a glance at me with his pathetic brown eyes. "And I tried to tell you before but then May came by.

I didn't want to make you feel worse than you already did when I wasn't sure. I'm sorry for waiting."

"If you'd said something sooner, it might have helped us to find my sister."

He tried to smile. "I'm helping now, aren't I?"

"No, you're not. You're a liar."

As I rushed past him, he yelled, "Why don't you ask Tony? Then you'll find out who the liar is."

"I will," I shouted back.

After school I went flying out the front door. I'd run into Debbie earlier, and she'd told me to meet her and Tony in the parking lot. I was in such a hurry to get there I didn't see May or Sheila until I practically ran into them.

"What did you do to your hair?" May said.

I hesitated. It probably wasn't a good idea to mention Tony. "I dyed it. I needed a change."

She smiled. "You did a pretty good job."

Sheila studied me. "It's the same color as May's, but it looks different on you. I'm not sure it goes with your eyes."

I frowned. "I've got to go. I'm on my way to meet Debbie."

Sheila patted her puffy dark hair. "What are you hanging out with her for?"

The way she said this made me want to scream. I was so tired of everyone saying bad things about the people who were trying to help me. "Because I want to."

"Does your mother know?" May adjusted her purse strap.

"Of course she does. I don't lie to her about everything," I said, though lately it seemed like I did.

"I can't believe she'd let you hang out with her," May said.

Sheila rolled her eyes and said to May, "Well, it is her mother."

"What do you mean?" I stammered.

May wrinkled the blank page of her forehead. "Caroline, it's no secret that your mom is having a little nervous breakdown right now. And the way she let Jess run around, some people are saying . . . ."

"What? What do they say?" I asked.

"We don't want to hurt your feelings." May's faux concern made me ill.

I took a deep breath. Sheila touched May's arm. "People are saying that if your mom didn't let Jess do whatever she wanted, she might not be missing now."

"It's not her fault." I could barely get the words out. "If anything, it's my fault." There was dead silence.

May touched my shoulder. "You can't blame yourself. Jess wasn't your responsibility." With her hand still on my shoulder, she added, "This may be hard to hear, but your mom should have checked on her when she didn't come home that night. Any normal mom would have."

I tore myself away. "If my mom is abnormal, then your dad must be abnormal, too, because he's always hanging around with her." I blurted it out before I even realized what I was implying.

"What do you mean?" May backed away slowly.

"You know what I mean." I tried to catch her eye. She had to have noticed the way her dad was always hovering around my mom, putting his arm around her waist, and whispering things to her. She had to know.

"Liar," May said, Sheila by her side. "Liar, liar, liar." She bent over and began to cry. Sheila glared at me as if I had just committed a terrible crime.

CHAPTER 16

"We almost left without you." Debbie leaned against Tony's car. He stood next to her, smoking a cigarette, looking cool in black jeans, a leather vest, and a tight T-shirt.

"I knew my girl wouldn't let me down." He winked at me.

It felt nice that he'd called me his girl, but I couldn't look at him without thinking of what Billy had told me.

Moose leaned out the window. "Can we get rolling already?"

"Now we can." Tony held the door open for me and I got in.

Debbie squeezed in front next to Moose with a smile. He turned the radio up, and took a swallow from a bottle of vodka. Debbie bobbed her head to the music in a robotic way. I sat all alone in the back seat as they passed the bottle between them up front. I hoped Tony wasn't going to drink and drive recklessly.

As if reading my thoughts, Debbie said, "Don't worry. I've been driving around with Tony a long time and nothing bad has ever happened. He's got angels watching over him."

"That's one way of putting it," Moose said with a grunt.

Tony cast a quick glance my way. "The thing is, once you don't fear death, it loses its power over you. You live life differently." He went on in a voice that was soft but so strong, it made me sit up and listen. "Death isn't any more important to me than it is to a bug that smashes on the windshield. It's just something that happens, like brushing your teeth or having a beer." My stomach churned.

"But maybe I feel that way because I've stared death down with my own two eyes. You others haven't been so fortunate."

"Would you stop going on like that? You're giving me the creeps," Moose said.

"I bet Caroline is interested," Tony said.

"I guess," I replied uneasily.

We hit a straightaway and he gunned the engine. The car took off like a rocket. He kept going faster and faster until I had to put my hands over my eyes.

He finally slowed down and said, "You don't live life at twenty-five miles an hour. Isn't that right, Caroline?" I was trembling too hard to answer.

When we pulled up in front of his house, everyone got out and headed through the gate. Tony put his hand on my arm and held me back. "Got a minute?" he asked. "I need to talk to you."

"About what?" I could see myself distorting in the lenses of his dark sunglasses.

He scratched his jaw. "About your sister."

"What about her?" I clutched my books tighter.

He pushed my hair from my sweaty face. "You still want to help me find her, don't you?" He rested his hand on my shoulder. What Billy had said made me want to pull away, but I needed Tony to help me find Jess.

He gave my shoulder a squeeze, and I remembered our kiss.

"I do," I said.

"Good." He paused. "My band is coming over and we're gonna play. I want you to stay and listen."

"What's the name of your band?" I asked.

He smiled slowly. "The Drown." He looked off into the distance, his face pale as a dream, and said, "Come on, let's go inside." As he slipped his arm around my waist, his hand grazed the skin under my shirt.

"Caroline!" Edie ran toward me like I was her long-lost friend and flung her arms around me. "We're having another party. We're gonna bake a cake. I have a mix."

Lizzie sat in a rocking chair, feeding her baby a bottle. Moose sat down on the couch and picked up a *Popular Mechanics* magazine. A guy I didn't know began talking to him. He smiled at me as if we were already best friends, and introduced himself as Peter. He had light hair and a shy manner that made him handsome in spite of his bad skin. For a second everything made sense—handsome with bad skin, he had to be the guy in the red car. But he couldn't be, because he was here.

"You look like Alice in Wonderland," he said. He made a courtly bow and swept the air with his arm. "At your service, beautiful lady." Then he and Moose began searching around in the fridge for something to eat. Tony and Debbie were by the fireplace, talking. Someone put on some music. It swirled around me as I leaned back on the couch, trying to relax.

Peter came back with a beer, plopped down on the couch next to me and said, "Hey, little sis, you're still here." Something about how he said this made me smile. It was like we were all part of a giant family, a family that didn't say terrible things every other minute, a family that didn't make me unhappy.

"Let's get pretty for the party," Edie said.

I glanced at Tony, trying to summon the courage to ask him about Billy. "Go on," he said.

Lizzie picked up her baby and we followed Edie into a bedroom that I assumed was Tony's. Lizzie put her baby down on the unmade double bed, and tucked her up beneath an Indian bedspread. As I put my books down beside the bed I noticed something that looked like a game board sticking out from under it.

Edie shouted, "Don't touch that," as I reached for it.

"What is it?" I said.

Edie hesitated then said, "It's a Ouija board. It's for talking to spirits, but that one has bad vibes."

I stepped back. Lizzie rolled her eyes. "And some people have crazy vibes."

"There, there." Edie leaned over and patted the baby's little head.

"What's her name?" I asked.

She laughed. "Lothlórien. It's from some stupid book that Lizzie loves."

Lizzie gave her a look, lit up a cigarette, and exhaled a plume of smoke. "God, I needed that. You have no idea how hard it is taking care of a baby."

"Who's the father?" I asked.

She bit her lower lip. "Someone who isn't around anymore."

"You got a boyfriend?" Edie said to me.

I shook my head. "I almost did."

"What happened?"

"We were together for a while." I wasn't sure one kiss constituted a while but I didn't know what else to say. "He left me for a friend of mine."

"What's his name?"

"Billy O'Neil. You probably don't know him."

"We know him," Lizzie said. I raised an eyebrow. "Tall, red hair, freckles, football player. And a pretty superior attitude for someone who doesn't know shit." She put special emphasis on that last part.

"You don't like him?" I said.

Lizzie shrugged. "I don't know him well enough to like him or not."

"Is he the one who comes to the wash to drink sometimes?" Edie asked.

"That would be him," Lizzie said.

I inhaled deeply. This was my chance. I had to say something. "Billy said he was at the wash the night Jess disappeared." Lizzie and Edie looked at each other. I went on, "It's probably not true, but he thinks he might have seen Tony driving Jess away from the wash. Is that even possible?"

Edie started to say, "It was kind of confusing that night . . . ."

Lizzie interrupted her, "Billy's a total loser, and he was so smashed that night, he was probably seeing double." My worries eased a little. She took another puff of her cigarette.

"You'll find someone better than him." Edie touched my shoulder. "Love doesn't have to do with any particular person. Where love is, love is." She looked almost beatific as she said this. I thought of her precious green ring in the white box, of how Tony was in love with Jess, and Edie was in love with him. And then I thought of Tony kissing me—the feeling impossible to doubt.

Lizzie eyed me. "Edie is such a romantic."

Edie scowled and began rifling through a pile of clothes next to the bed. "There's some nice stuff here. Want to try something on? I love switching around clothes with people." She held up a denim dress with madras pockets and a zipper with a big ring on it going down the front. I shook my head. The thought of wearing some stranger's clothes grossed me out.

"What about this?"

My jaw dropped. She held up a lime-green dress with a white collar, white cuffs on the short sleeves, and a white belt.

"Is something wrong?" she asked. "It will look good on you."

I reached for it and brought it to my face. There was the faint flower scent of the deodorant my sister used. "I think this is Jess's dress."

Lizzie said, "Jesus. We didn't know."

"She must have left it here a while ago. Lots of people leave clothes here. No one minds if we wear them." Edie's eyes searched my face. I started to hand it back, but she stopped me. "You should wear it. With your blonde hair, you look just like her."

"I guess I do." The green of the dress seemed to jump out at me.

"I don't think she'd mind if you wore it," Edie said.

I put it on carefully, my heart beating too hard the whole time as I struggled with the hooks and the back zipper. Edie put on the denim dress, and Lizzie chose a purple velvet dress with a sequined collar.

"I love dressing up," Edie said. "Just the other day some guy told me I could be a model."

"Yeah, Edie, like that's true." Lizzie rolled her eyes.

Edie frowned. "He even took some pictures. He said I remind him of Twiggy, and he would know. He's worked with her." I'd seen pictures of Twiggy in magazines. Her hair was cut as short as a boy's, but, like Edie, she was thin as a stick and had huge eyes with mile-long lashes.

Lizzie shook her head and looked at me. "It's funny. You can't believe a word she says, but Edie believes everything everyone tells her."

She scowled. I pulled the white belt tight. The top was a little big, but the dress had a full skirt that made me want to twirl. It would look good with Jess's white pumps. I thought of their soft leather, the white roses and delicate ankle straps, and imagined myself dancing in them, my footsteps so light they'd barely touch the ground. It felt strange and wrong to be thinking this now, and yet wearing my sister's dress was magical, as if with each rustling of the material I could hear her breathless whisper.

Edie picked up a makeup bag from a table by the bed, took out some green eye shadow, and brushed it on my eyes.

"Like Cleopatra," she said. She found some small round iridescent stickers in the bag.

"Put one on your forehead," she said. "They're reflectors." Lizzie and I both did. We stood there, the three of us with shining circles on our brows.

"We're stars," Edie said.

Tony was fooling with the cord to his electric guitar when we walked in. A couple of other guys were on the makeshift stage, setting up the amps. When he saw me, Tony dropped the cord on the floor. He pushed his hand through his hair and stared.

"Jesus," he said. "Where did you get that dress?"

I smoothed the skirt. Could he hate it that much? "It was in the bedroom. Edie gave it to me."

He ran his hands along my shoulders and said, "Jesus," again.

"I can change if you want me to."

"No, please don't change," he said. "Jess must have left that dress here a while ago."

I clutched the green cloth. "That's what Edie said."

He sighed. "She always left stuff here." He picked up his guitar and strummed a chord. I still had so many questions, but I could tell he didn't want to talk right now.

More people were in the living room. I didn't know any of them except for Debbie. She sat at one end of the couch, wearing fishnet stockings, and looking like the most bored person in the universe. Some of the others were kids who went to football games and cheered at rallies. There were a few of the arty drama club kids too, and some kids from the tough crowd at school. I'd always thought of Tony as part of that crowd, but it was like he was bringing all these different types of kids together. And the one thing everyone seemed to have in common was they couldn't take their eyes off of me and him. I wasn't sure why. Did they hate me? Did they think the two of us were strange? I was relieved when Lizzie came up, took his hand and led him out to the pool.

Edie said, "Let's bake that cake now."

We discovered two cake pans at the back of a cupboard. They had cobwebs in them. Even after I washed them, they still looked gross. We had no frosting but Edie said Tony probably would buy some for us. I smiled. It was like he was the dad. The only thing wrong was that Jess wasn't here. I imagined her returning, moving through the crowded room in her easy, graceful way. She would be the most beautiful one of all. With a weeping ache inside, I thought that she should be standing here with Tony in this dress. I wouldn't mind. They were meant for each other—even their recklessness was alike. And I would be so grateful to have her home.

As we were stirring the cake mix, Tony came back in and reached his arms around my waist. Edie gave him a hurt look.

"How's it going, girls?" he asked.

"Fine until you interrupted." Edie pouted. "So what were you and Lizzie talking about?"

"The usual. She was worried about getting the baby home. I told her Moose would give her and the baby a ride later."

"You always take my friends away." She gave me a look and stomped off.

Tony stared at me. "That girl drives me crazy." He smiled as though something was amusing. "And Caroline, just letting you know, you can't believe everything your loser ex-lover-boy tells you."

I gasped. "What are you talking about?"

"Word gets around." He tapped the reflector on my forehead. "Your buddy Billy has a big mouth. He's been talking trash about me."

"What did he say?"

He sighed. "Things I'd rather not repeat. But I know better than to believe a word he says. I hope you do, too."

I nodded. "He's always telling me not to hang out with you. I guess he doesn't like you."

Tony shook his head. "I'm not one of those puppet people, always worried about what other people think. I've got to be myself, and if that means some people hate me, I don't care. Jess never cared about stuff like that, either." He looked hard at me. "Is that all Billy said?"

I shook my head. I had to tell him. My voice shook as I spoke. "He said he thought he saw you with Jess in your car the night of the party, and that she was screaming."

He stared at me. "I have no idea why he would say something hurtful like that, unless . . . ." He ground the toe of his boot in the rug. "He's referring to when I drove her back to my house to get her purse. She left it there when we stopped off before the party. You know Jess. She had to have it. Probably needed the money for California."

Though I could see Jess insisting on that, it still didn't make sense. I couldn't let it go. I needed to know. "But Billy said she was screaming."

"She was mad at me because of Edie, but she wasn't screaming." He sighed. "Maybe Billy got a little creative with the truth so he could turn you against me. Can you think why he'd want to do that?"

"Because he still likes me." I guessed that was possible.

"Yup. Guys always want what they can't have." Tony smiled. "Tell me if he bothers you, and I'll take care of him." He hesitated, then took my hands in his and said, "You okay?"

He looked at me so tenderly I almost cried with gratitude. For once someone was watching out for me. As he started practicing with the band, I wrapped my arms around myself, desperately wanting what he'd told me to be true.

CHAPTER 17

Jangling electric chords pierced the air, punctuated every now and then by drumrolls. Edie tapped me on the shoulder. "You know what would make this a lot more fun? Getting high."

"What?" I said.

"Don't tell me you've never gotten high." When I told her I hadn't, she said, "I have to see you high." She grabbed my hand and took me out to the pool. There were kids all around, but they didn't even notice us. Something about the way they stood together talking, smoking, staring, made me feel like I was part of something bigger than I was, bigger than all of us. I felt a surge of excitement.

Edie lit up a joint, inhaled, and handed it to me. It smelled really bad.

"Maybe not," I said.

She frowned. "It's only pot." She guided the joint to my lips. "Trust me. You're just gonna feel a little happy."

I inhaled and coughed violently. It was like I'd swallowed fire.

"That wasn't so bad, was it?" Edie said.

"No," I replied, still coughing. She handed it back to me a bunch more times. Nothing was really happening yet, but finally I told Edie I didn't want any more. Much as I liked reading about drugs, I was feeling a little anxious.

She frowned. "This is Moose's. It's good shit. But suit yourself. All the more for me." When she'd finished the joint we went back inside. The murmur of the crowd was like bees buzzing. Everything grew distant. It was like the world was spinning away from me. Edie hovered over Tony as he tuned his guitar. Debbie leaned against the fireplace mantel, smoking a cigarette, and talking to Peter, who was gesturing wildly. Lizzie was rocking her baby. I couldn't make out what anyone was saying. Except for the surreal humming in the background, it was like a silent movie. Everyone had someone to talk to except me. I began counting the small blue flowers that patterned the wallpaper, numerous as stars. Though probably only a few minutes had passed, it felt like I'd been standing there forever.

Edie grabbed my arm, shaking me from my dream. "Oh my God, we forgot the cake," she said. The batter was still sitting in the bowl. As she was pouring it into the pans, she didn't even notice that she'd missed, and was spilling it on the kitchen counter. That really cracked us up.

She scooped some up with her finger and licked it off. "Want to know a secret?"

I caught my breath. "What?"

She smiled. "I like cake better before it's cooked." We both cracked up again, then poured the rest into the pans. While it was baking, we drank Coke and ate Cheez-Its. Nothing had ever tasted so good. When the cake was almost done, Edie peeked in the oven. It had risen over the tops of the pans and rolled down the sides onto the bottom of the oven.

"It's the cake that took over the world," she said, and we laughed some more. I'd never laughed so hard. She put her pale hand on my arm. "We really can't cook, can we?" she said, and the way she said "we" almost made me cry. My faraway feeling had left and I hadn't even noticed.

Moose came over, plopped his big paw-like hand on Edie's shoulder and said, "Gimme some cake, woman."

"It's not ready, you big dope." She extricated herself from his hand. He gazed at her adoringly and lumbered off. She said, "Moose gives me the creeps."

"Why?" I asked.

She shrugged. "He was in jail, you know."

"What for?"

"Rape, murder, shoplifting, who the fuck knows," she said, and though this wasn't funny at all, we both started laughing *again*. "The worst thing is he likes me." She made a face. "And he follows me around like he's trying to protect me or something. Can you imagine?"

I shook my head. "Does Tony mind?"

She sucked on her little finger. "Tony doesn't mind." She looked at me. "He knows I'm his girl."

Kids grabbed handfuls of cake from the pan. It was gone before I knew it. Edie convinced me to smoke another joint and we drank some red wine from a gallon jug. I felt like I was at the party and somewhere else at the same time. One minute I'd be listening to the people near me; the next I could swear I heard a conversation that wasn't at the party. Someone said, "Caroline," in a loud whisper and when I turned there was no one there. It was like I was caught between two worlds. Panic rose up inside of me. I stared down at the green dress. The shadows in the creases were like valleys, and the starlight pale folds like mountains. It was the most beautiful thing I'd ever seen; a country all its own, with clouds, sheep bell tinkles, and silver ponds. Jess country. I could see her stepping on the pond that was now a frozen mirror. She was skating on the ice mirror, her white lace-up skates making soundless figure eights. Everything was spinning, like she was. I had to sit down, but where? It was like Jess was really here, next to me, her hand on mine. For a second I was sure I heard her say, "How's it going, sis," and felt the hiss of her warm breath on my ear. But she wasn't here. She was gone. My pulse was racing. I wanted to go home. And the worst thing was Tony had disappeared, too. I tried to steady myself and ended up flopping down on the couch next to Debbie, who scratched her leg and refused to acknowledge my existence.

"Wake up," Edie said. "The band is starting to play."

"I thought they were already done." Time had gotten all mixed up, almost as if there was no time.

"Don't be silly. It's only been a few minutes since we ate the cake."

"Oh." I tried to calm my nerves. Was I going crazy like my mother? Edie's smile wasn't reassuring. She looked like someone wearing an Edie mask. Debbie was wearing a Debbie mask, too, right down to her pig-like, gray eyes.

Then Tony strolled in and the world fell back into place. There was something beautiful about the way he moved, as if he owned the room. A chill went through me. I imagined it went through everyone else as well. The other band members stood behind him. I felt a surge of pride as he put one leg on the amp, leaned his guitar on it and strummed a piercing chord. He was so handsome in his tight black pants, his hair falling in his eyes. He and the band members had painted their faces white and darkened their eyes. He looked like a mime. Everyone was staring at him, but he was looking at me. It was just one quick blue glance, but I saw it.

"This here's a little song I wrote for someone special," he said. I couldn't suppress a smile, but I noticed Edie couldn't, either. He began singing about rain in his heart, darkness in the rain. His liquid dark voice washed over us. The other members of the band joined in. It was so loud it gave me the shivers. Edie, Peter,

Moose, Debbie, Lizzie, everyone in the room was watching him, but I couldn't shake the sense he was singing directly to me. He had the whole room in the palm of his hand, but the music was for me, and I felt its power. It was a black velvet river, like nothing I'd ever touched before. I shut my eyes, aware of the world within, the world outside me, and the strange beauty of everything.

The band launched into a faster, hard-driving song about a train. It was barreling through my mind when someone tapped me on the shoulder. Startled, I turned to see that it was Tony. He'd stepped away from the band, though they were still playing.

"Want to dance?" he said. Before I could answer, he'd taken my hands in his. I gulped. I wasn't a very good dancer, but he was. His feet moved so fast, I couldn't keep up. He pulled me to him, his arm tight around my waist, and then spun me around. When the song ended I bent over, out of breath. He lifted my chin.

"I don't know how to dance as well as Jess," I said.

He shook his head. "You just need her dancing shoes."

I looked up at him. "Dancing shoes?" I was wearing my new patent leather school shoes. Their chunky heels were heavy, not light.

"Those pretty white ones she used to wear with that dress." He ran his finger down my arm. "I found one in the bedroom the other day, but I couldn't find the other." His sad gaze met mine.

"That's funny. I found one in our room." I paused. "I was just thinking of them." It was as if we really were connected in some special way.

"She must have brought it here that night when she wanted to go dancing, but left one at home by mistake. She could be forgetful."

I nodded. "Sounds just like her."

"It broke my heart when I found it." A weary look crossed his face and then he went back to play with the band.

It was dark when they finished playing. The pot and wine were wearing off. Edie and Debbie were talking to Tony. When I walked up, he turned to me. "We're gonna move this party to the desert. You in?"

I told him I was going to be in a lot of trouble if I didn't leave soon.

He shook his head. "Jess wouldn't have left."

I shrugged. "And she always got in trouble."

Tony looked at me sadly. "If you really have to go, I'll give you a ride."

"Can I come?" Edie asked.

He turned to her. "No."

She looked hurt.

I began backing away. "I have to get my books," I said.

Edie watched with forlorn brown eyes as Tony followed me into the bedroom. I grabbed my books from beside the bed. He stood next to me, a little too close. As I fumbled with the books, a notebook fell on the floor. He picked it up and pulled out "Death and the Buttercup." Mr. Raymond's glowing comments about my talent for poetry were written across the top. I could have died.

He sat down on the bed and held the poem close to his face. His mascara had smeared on the white makeup, making gray shadows under his eyes. He looked like some unreal being reading it. "That's some cool stuff, Caroline."

I nodded.

"But it doesn't sound like you."

"What do you mean?"

"Sounds like someone older."

I asked him to give it back.

"Sit down," he said. I sat down next to him. One of the sheets was coming off the mattress. They were grayish white—not pink like the ones Mom stretched tightly on my bed—and they smelled different, too. My sheets always smelled like flower perfume. These smelled like cigarettes and sweat.

Tony reached his arm around my shoulder. I didn't move. My hand was touching the bare mattress. And then he kissed me. It was as if we were both reaching toward something I couldn't name, except to say I wanted more of it. My skin felt fuzzy. He undid the zipper of the green dress, gently peeled it off my shoulders. He paused for a moment, looking at me, and all the feelings from this summer welled up inside me. I thought I might cry. We lay back on the bed. He traced his finger along the lace of my bra.

"Am I going too fast for you?" His strange mask-face was looking at me, but at the same time it was like he was looking at something miles away. "'Cause if you want me to stop, I will." As he pulled his shirt off, for one crazy second I wanted to brush my lips against the small blue star tattooed on his pale bicep, but I didn't. He pressed my hand against his stomach. I could feel the hard muscles beneath his downy skin. His expression became dreamy. I pulled my hand away.

I said, "Jess wouldn't want me to do this."

"Wherever love is, love is," he said sadly.

"I don't understand."

"I'm sorry. I guess I got you confused with someone else." He looked away. When he turned back to me I felt an ache inside. Had I done something wrong? I was so hopeless. I never did the right thing.

"I can't help that I'm different from Jess." I touched his smooth shoulder.

"You don't have to be like her. You just have to be you." He pushed my hair away from my face. He repeated, "You." He kissed me again, ran his hands up under my bra, his palms warm and rough. His eyes had the look of blue flowers wilted in the heat and something else I didn't understand. It was almost as if he was someone I didn't know, someone warm, cold, and mysterious, all at the same time. It must have been the white makeup. I was so lost in what I was feeling I almost didn't hear the door open. I looked up. Edie was hovering on the threshold, thin and pale like a ghost, her small hand clutching the doorframe as she stared at us with eyes as wide as saucers.

"What is it?" Tony said, annoyed.

"I was just, just." She was like a record stuck on the same note.

"Get out," Tony said, and she fled. "That girl, she's like a cat. Every time I turn around, she's there."

"She just likes you," I said.

"I guess that's it." He rolled his eyes. "Where did we leave off?"

"I have to go," I said. "It's late. My parents will kill me."

"I forgot you were still a little schoolgirl. I'll drive you home." He stroked me under the chin and smiled as he said, "Death and the Buttercup."

"I have to change first." I looked down at the dress, hanging half off me. "It would send my parents over the edge to see me in this."

He stared back at me as if this were the saddest thing.

I went on, "My mom cries all the time, and when she isn't crying, she's mean as a snake. And my dad is . . . ." I paused, not wanting to say this, but having to. "A drunk. Sometimes it's like I don't even have parents anymore."

"Parents. Who needs them?" He shook his head. "Go ahead, change."

I frowned. "Can you please leave?"

"Sure." As he stood in the doorway he said, "And Caroline?"

"What?"

"Someday, if you're a good girl, I'll show you *my* poetry."

I wanted to believe that we had this in common, but I wasn't sure. He didn't look like a poet to me in his black boots and tight jeans, but I figured with someone like Tony, you could never tell.

I was zipping up my denim skirt when Edie walked in. She glared at me.

"I'm sorry," I said.

"You'll be sorrier later," she replied.

"What do you mean?"

She sat down so close to me I could smell her wine breath. "He killed a girl, you know."

My blood froze.

"Jess?" I was barely able to speak her name.

She shook her head. "No, some other girl. She's buried somewhere in the desert. He killed her and he didn't even care, and I shouldn't be telling you this 'cause he'd kill *me* if he knew I'd told you."

She stared at me coldly. I wanted to leave, but the way she was looking at me made it impossible to move. "You're lying," I said. "You just want me to give him up so you can have him back, but the truth is neither of us can have him. He loves my sister."

She didn't flinch. "Believe what you want, but I'm telling you the truth." Her skinny fingers absent-mindedly toyed with the big ring on the zipper that went down the front of her dress. Her pupils were so large, her eyes looked like black holes. She didn't seem like Edie anymore. She seemed like someone who'd taken too many drugs.

"How do you know it's the truth?" I asked.

She touched the small scar by her lip. "The ghost from the Ouija board told me."

"You're crazy," I said. "Abnormal."

"Ready?" a voice said.

We turned to see Tony standing in the doorway.

CHAPTER 18

Tony and I stopped by the pool before going to the car. Light reflecting from the house shimmered on the water. He took my books from me and put them on the ground. Then he took my hand, and I knew I should be afraid of him, but I wasn't. It didn't seem possible that he'd killed someone. Edie lied about everything. Everyone knew that, but I couldn't get her words out of my head.

He turned to me, his glance soft as a breeze. "You know what I like about you?"

"What?"

"You listen. No one else listens." He put his arm around me. "I miss her. God, I miss her."

He led me closer to the edge. Our two reflections blended in the water, his sad shadow touching mine. "I've been told I'm an old soul." He paused. "I'm not so sure about that, but sometimes I do feel like I'm living in the wrong time, like I don't belong here."

I squeezed his hand. "Me too." I remembered what Jess had said about his loneliness. I felt it now. It was like a darkness reaching into space and touching me at the same time. He'd washed off the white makeup, but there were still smudges beneath his eyes. He looked like he hadn't slept in weeks. His hair was damp and messed up. I could tell that he was suffering. Now wasn't the time to ask him about what Edie had said. If it wasn't true, it would hurt him. He wouldn't trust me anymore and he might stop helping me. And if it was true . . . . I didn't want to think about that. I needed to listen, watch, and wait for the right time to ask, the way detectives did on TV. I stepped back from the water.

"Come on," he said, and we went over to the car and got in. I sat on the far end of the front seat, but he pulled me close. I was so confused. He turned on the radio. Marianne Faithfull sang "As Tears Go By." Her voice was breathy, soft, and beautiful. It was like she was singing of my sadness, our sadness.

"You like this?" he said. I nodded. His eyes searched my face. "I knew you would."

He drove more slowly this time, the headlights illumining the road a little ahead, the rest swallowed by darkness. Much as I wanted to ignore them, Edie's words still weighed on me. I was resisting the urge to ask when he said, "I have a confession to make."

I almost jumped out of my seat.

He went on, "I do know the guy who drove Jess to California."

"What?"

"His name is Brian Glen. He's a pal of mine. When I saw how mad your sister was and how determined she was to run off to California, I asked him to take her. I knew he'd keep an eye on her and let me know where she was when they got there."

"So you knew where she was all this time and you didn't say anything?" My voice was shaking. "I thought we were a team, and we were going to share what we knew."

"That's why I wanted to see you today. I was just waiting to be sure she was okay before I told you. Brian called me last night." He cleared his throat. "Seems Jess told him she hated me and never wanted to speak to me again." He looked away. "But when Brian saw a story about her in the news, he decided to call. He said she's staying with him in Redondo Beach."

This was too strange. "Redondo Beach? My dad looked for Jess there, but he didn't find her."

He smiled. "That's 'cause he's your dad."

I paused, letting his words sink in. "Are you sure Jess is in California?" He nodded. "But what if your friend is lying?"

He frowned. "Brian doesn't lie."

I stared at him, finding it hard to accept this incredible truth. "You sure?"

"I'm as sure of this as I am of that moon in the sky."

As I gazed up at the giant white disc hanging over us in all its majesty, I wanted so much to believe that Jess was somewhere and that all these weeks of waiting might finally be over, that she wasn't—I could barely think the word—dead. "So how are you going to get her to come home?" I asked.

He laughed. "I think you mean what are we going to do to get her home? We, you and me, we're going to California, and we're going to find her. We're a team. Remember?"

"We're both going to California?"

He nodded. "You have to come. She hates me right now, but she doesn't hate you."

"But shouldn't we tell the police so they can find her?"

He looked at me. "You know that won't work. Jess is like a butterfly. You've got to creep up real quiet, or she'll fly off. Sometimes people who run away don't want to be found, but I think she'd let you find her."

What he said made a lot of sense. "When should we go?"

"Soon. We'll just take off like in *On the Road*." As he turned into the neighborhood where I lived, he gestured toward all the little box houses and said, "And leave these puppet people living their phony little lives behind."

"But I have school," I said.

He frowned. "Caroline, we're talking about finding Jess here. Isn't that more important than school?"

"I guess." I bit my nail. I was happy, but at the same time the thought of actually getting in Tony's car and leaving my family behind as we sped down the highway on our way to California made me nervous.

He gazed through the windshield, not smiling. I wanted him to squeeze my hand to reassure me, but he just kept driving. I worried that I'd disappointed him. He pulled up about a block from my house, as always. I was about to get out of the car when he pressed a piece of paper into my hand. I looked at him questioningly.

"That's my poem." He smiled. I started to open it but he said, "Don't read it now. And don't tell anyone about California, okay?" I nodded. As I gathered up my books, he added, "You don't have to do anything you don't want to do, but remember, Jess might move around. I don't know how much longer she'll be in Redondo." He touched his finger to his lips and then touched mine.

Upstairs, in the light from the lamp with the pink-flowered shade, I unfolded the piece of paper. On it was written:

There is darkness in the rain.
Darkness touching every living thing.
Darkness on the other side of the moon.
Each drop like a silver knife penetrates my dream.
Tears apart the earth.
Takes a soul downstream.
I swim up out of the darkness away from all the pain.
I am resurrected in the rain.

Though I didn't completely understand his poem, I was relieved. How could someone who'd written something as beautiful as this have done what Edie said? As I smoothed out the paper and placed it on my desk, I wondered if Tony felt the same way I did, that poetry was one of the only things that could get him through all of this.

When he didn't call for days, I ricocheted between excitement and fear. Doubts arose at the oddest moments. I'd be spreading mayonnaise on bread when the phrase "he killed someone" would go through my mind, and I'd lose my appetite. Then I'd remind myself that Edie was a liar who was full of crazy ideas that she got from a Ouija board, for Christ's sake, and I knew where Jess was. I was going to find her.

Other times I'd wake in the middle of the night thinking that precious time was passing, and we had to go to California right away. I'd clutch the sheet and as I inhaled its flower scent, the doughy smell of Tony's sheets would come back to me.

The hardest part was not telling my parents about any of this. Every time I looked into their faces, I could see how upset they were, but I couldn't forget what Tony had said about Jess being like a butterfly. I couldn't tell them she was in California. I'd already messed up by not telling them she'd snuck out. If I did something that made us lose her again, I wouldn't be able to live with myself.

On Wednesday afternoon, I sat in the white chair that went with my white desk, trying to do my history homework, but I couldn't concentrate. I went to the window, pushed aside the curtains, and tapped my fingers on the glass. The longer we waited to go to California, the greater the likelihood was that Jess would slip away. She'd never been patient. Why wouldn't Tony call?

Had something happened to him? If Jess were in my place, she'd be bombarding him with phone calls by now. She went after what she wanted so easily. But every time I thought of picking up the phone I froze, unable to summon the courage to do it.

From outside I heard the muffled jingle of the ice cream truck. It pulled up across the street. Kids came streaming out of nowhere, and formed a line. I wished I was one of those kids, standing in line for ice cream, but that time was as far away as the twinkle of a distant star.

I sat down on the rug, wrapped my arms around my knees, and stared at the pink phone, wishing I could make it ring. The only way I could ever figure things out was if Tony called me. And then, as if it heard my wish, the phone really did ring, its sound lovelier even than the ice cream truck's jingle. Before anyone else in the house could answer, I picked it up. It was Tony. I felt a rush from head to toe.

He said, "Did you get a chance to read my poem?"

"Yes." I hoped he wasn't going to ask what I thought it meant, because I had trouble explaining things like that.

"I got a thing about the water." There was a silence. "How it changes you. I almost drowned once, you know."

"Someone told me that."

"There's probably more to it than you heard, but I don't want to bore you with the details."

"I don't mind listening," I said.

"Okay." He took a deep breath. "I was at Sabino Canyon. It had been raining hard, and the creek bed rose. Some of my friends dared me to jump over it, and you know me. I did and I missed, but I didn't scream for help. I laughed."

"You laughed?"

"I did. The water was churning all around me, dragging me downstream, and I just let go. It was exciting to be so helpless. As I went under I thought my chest was going to explode, but then I got this feeling of peace and everything went black, and I saw the nothing that is beneath all of us. And it was infinite." Infinite, I thought. Just like in my book.

He paused. "When I opened my eyes, I was a new person."

"You mean you're not really you?"

His voice grew serious. "No, Caroline. Now I'm the real me. It's hard to understand unless it happens to you. I should have died, but I didn't. And now, unlike most of the stupid people stuck on this planet, I'm not afraid to live my life. I'm not afraid to do anything because I know there's no past, no future. There's only now." He paused to let me absorb that. "People said it was an accident but it wasn't. What happened wasn't like all the bullshit they talk about in the Bible, either. It was magic."

"I believe in magic," I said quietly. "I think there are moments when you can pass from one world into another. When the edges of things are soft. Like an amoeba. If you find one of them, anything is possible." I wrapped the cord around my wrist. "Those moments are like a door. You just have to figure out how to open it. Some people do it with drugs. For you, maybe it was drowning."

"Then I guess we have that in common." He paused. "Doors and amoebas. You never cease to surprise me."

I wanted to say more, but I worried I'd said too much.

"You okay?" he finally asked.

"Yes. Thanks for calling."

"You sure are a thankful girl," he said. "Do you thank everyone for everything?"

"No."

"Good, 'cause I have more to say." I went over and pushed the window up. It felt stuffy in my room. "Caroline?"

"Yes." I stretched the cord as far as it would go, leaned my head out, and looked down below. For some reason I expected to see his car, but it wasn't there. The dusty gray-green leaves of the mesquite tree were like almond-shaped eyes watching me.

"Remember how I said we'd figure out when to go to California?"

"Yes." Billy stepped outside and dragged a trashcan to the edge of his yard.

"Well, we need to go now."

Now? Billy waved to me, then pulled both his eyes down with his fingers and made a goofy face. He was like a small clay figure standing down there, a perfect imitation of Billy. I said, "But I can't just leave after all my parents have been through this summer."

"I'm going to ask you something," he said. "What would make your parents' lives worse—you leaving for a few days and coming back with Jess, or you not leaving and maybe never seeing your sister again? Think about it."

It would only be for a few days. The thought of being in a car alone with Tony thrilled me, but at the same time it made my breath come too fast, the way it often did before I panicked. "Are you really sure she's there?"

"Yes." He sounded almost angry.

"I don't know," I said. "This is all so sudden." I had to go if it meant finding my sister, but Edie's words still haunted me.

"Caroline, is something wrong?" he said.

I thought of asking him about Edie, but decided to keep it to myself a while longer.

"Look, I've had doubts too," he said. "I was worried Brian was lying to me, but he just sent me a photo of Jess from Redondo Beach."

My fears eased. "Can I see it?"

"Come out with me tonight. I'll show it to you then."

I unwound the cord from my wrist. "I don't think my parents will let me go out. It's a school night."

He sighed. "You always have an excuse. I guess you're afraid to live your own life. Jess wasn't like that. Just make something up for your parents. It's not that hard."

I hated that he thought of me this way.

He went on, "She needs you to be brave."

He was right. "Okay," I said.

"I'll pick you up at eight around the corner, where I always drop you off. We'll get something to eat, and we'll figure out how to get Jess home."

"See you then." I bounced up and down on my heels, finally allowing myself to feel excited. The lies were falling away and one thing was becoming clear. I was very close to finding my sister.

"And Caroline . . . ."

"What?"

"You never told me if you liked my poem."

I hesitated. "I liked it. I could really feel the sad darkness in it."

"I knew you'd like it. See you tonight." He paused. "And bring that white shoe. I'll bring the other one. We'll go dancing, just the way Jess wanted to." There was a touch of sorrow in his voice.

After putting the phone down carefully in the cradle where it fit so neatly, I ran back to the window. Though I knew I couldn't tell anyone about the photo, I was so excited I wanted to tell everyone. I looked down below again. Billy was gone.

CHAPTER 19

I was turning around when the Beckhams' sleek white car pulled up out front. Mom ran out and got in. I held my breath as she leaned her head toward Ron's. They sat side by side, like two silhouettes on a greeting card. I folded my arms across my chest in disgust. The worst thing was the smile on her face as she'd gotten in the car, as if she was happy to be driving away.

I opened up my history book, but after talking to Tony, it was boring and irrelevant. There was no point to learning about the past. There was only now. It was amazing that Tony was so handsome and also so wise. Jess had never mentioned this about him. Maybe he'd only shared these thoughts with me.

About ten minutes later I heard a car door slam shut and went back to the window. Mom was walking toward the house, carrying something wrapped in foil. She stopped and waved to Ron. He leaned his ugly tanned face out and smiled at her before driving away.

Right before supper, I went downstairs to give Mom my excuse. She was at the sink, peeling potatoes. She turned around. "You look happy."

I sat down. "Just taking a homework break." I lifted the foil from the package on the table.

"Don't touch that. That's one of Betty's spice cakes. We're having it for dessert."

I pressed the foil back down. "It was nice of Ron to deliver it."

She wiped her hands on her skirt. "He was in the neighborhood."

I stared at her. "If he was just bringing the cake, why did you go for a ride with him?"

"Caroline, were you spying on me?"

"Looking out the window isn't spying."

She sighed. "Ron and I drove around so he could talk to me in private about some things."

"Things about Jess?" I tore off a tiny piece of foil and rolled it into a ball.

She turned to me, her hands on her hips. "No. Things about you."

I smoothed the foil on my palm, imagining it was a silver leaf. "What things?"

She sat down at the table, and turned my face gently to her. "May told Ron that you were getting involved with the wrong crowd, Tony's crowd. She said you were doing it so you could find Jess."

"It isn't true." I frowned. What made May think she could meddle in my life like this?

"It's not your responsibility to find your sister." She picked up a spoon from the table, rubbed something off it with her finger.

"I'm not trying to find her," I said.

She touched my arm. I could smell her almond-vanilla hand lotion. "I don't know why May would lie."

I pulled away. "Maybe because I told her that you and Ron are in love."

She pushed her chair back. "What is wrong with you, Caroline?"

"Nothing." I stood up.

"Do you have any idea how you're making me feel?" She stared at me accusingly.

I shook my head. "No, I have no idea."

Her mouth tightened. With each passing second I felt further away from her, and I didn't care. All I wanted was to leave, but I still had to ask her about going out tonight. "Mom?" She looked up. "I'm sorry I said that."

Her expression softened. "Caroline, Ron is my friend. He's helping me get through all of this. Your dad and I, sometimes we're too upset to help each other." She pushed her hands through her hair. "There are a lot of things you don't understand. You can't just jump to conclusions. People will get hurt." She looked away.

I waited a moment then said, "I need to go over Billy's to work on a math project tonight, okay?"

She put the cake on the counter under a glass dome. "After what May said, I don't know."

"Mom, I'm going to fail math if I don't. And Billy's *my* friend."

She studied me. "All right, but I swear to God, Caroline Galvin, if I catch you having anything to do with Tony, I will ground you for the rest of your life. I'll send you away if I have to. I couldn't handle it if anything happened to you. I just couldn't."

I told myself to count to ten and swallowed hard. "I will never speak to Tony again." I stared at the clock. Thank God I'd be out of here in a couple of hours.

"Good." She brushed some crumbs off the counter with a sponge.

As I was opening the door into the hall, she looked up at me. Though I knew it was impossible, I couldn't shake the sense that she saw my secrets. I smiled nervously. Not that long ago, I might have told her all of them, but now I couldn't tell her anything.

So as not to raise suspicions, I didn't dress up to meet Tony. I only did small things that Mom wouldn't notice, like putting on extra deodorant and painting my nails lavender. I put on blush, but no lipstick. Mom definitely would have noticed that.

As I stood in the hall waiting to leave, all my sweet memories of kissing Tony were jammed up inside me, and much as I wanted to relive them, I couldn't feel a thing. My mouth was dry and tasted bad. I hoped Tony wouldn't hate my breath. Every part of me was on edge. Mom and Dad were still in the kitchen, drinking and arguing as they often did after supper now.

I was about to casually lean in and tell them I was on my way to Billy's when I heard Mom say, "Maybe we should send her to private school." I shuddered.

"Do we really have to do that?" Dad said.

"I will not sit back and lose another one of my daughters," Mom said.

"Frances, stop being so melodramatic."

"Jack, Ron said she's hanging out with Tony."

Dad said, "I suppose private school is Ron's idea, too. Do we have to do everything he says?"

I flattened myself against the wall. A cupboard door slammed. I bit my lip so hard I tasted blood. I'd run away before I let them send me to private school.

As I tiptoed down the hall, I heard Mom say, "Of course, after what happened with Jess back east, maybe it's not a good idea to send Caroline away to school."

"Caroline is not Jess," Dad said. "If you listened to her half as much as you listened to Ron, you'd know that."

I couldn't take this anymore, and went out to sit on the front step. I'd been jealous when my parents had sent Jess to that private school, but now it made me cringe to hear Mom say she was thinking of doing the same thing with me, as if I were broken, too, and needed to be fixed. Mom and Dad had been so optimistic about sending Jess there. They'd gone on and on about how great it would be for her, how impressive its drama program was. As usual, they got way ahead of themselves and were already imagining Jess on Broadway or in Hollywood before she'd even started. But she didn't get a part in any of the school plays, and ended up hanging lights. On opening night she and some boy stole whiskey from a liquor store, and he got arrested. They both were expelled. She'd lasted only three months. Of course, my parents smoothed everything over so she didn't have to go to court or anything. They didn't even punish her, unless you consider moving across the country a punishment. But that didn't work, either. This past year she'd gotten in trouble for stealing things from girls at school—a sweater, a gold watch. My parents didn't understand what they could be doing wrong.

I used to blame my sister for everything, but now I wondered if only Mom hadn't encouraged her foolish dreams she might have lasted longer at that school, if only my parents had punished her even once she might have changed her ways, if only she'd been more patient she might not have taken off for California. And if only she'd come back, she wouldn't always be an unfinished person in my mind. When I returned with her, things would be different. Maybe she would even be different. Maybe she'd be a person you could talk about without saying "if only."

"Oh, there you are." I almost jumped as Dad stepped out. "We were looking for you."

"I was about to go to Billy's to study."

The smoke from his cigarette uncoiled in the air. "Need a ride?" he said.

I glared at him. "Dad, he lives across the street."

He sat down on the step next to me. "Mind if I sit with you?"

I sighed. "I've got to go."

He staggered to his feet. "Sorry, kitten. I completely understand. Enjoy studying." In spite of his efforts to seem dignified, he stumbled as he headed back inside, and let the screen door bang behind him. I waited a second, then bolted down the street. When

I got to the place around the corner where Tony and I always met, I was out of breath. I became more and more anxious with each passing second, but when his car slowed to a stop in front of me, my nervousness melted away.

He leaned out, his white shirt untucked, a gold cross hanging around his neck. I could smell his musky cologne.

"You look beautiful," he said as I got inside. He smiled and kissed me as if this was something we did every day. He even touched my tongue with his, but I didn't mind. Everything about him seemed bigger, as if before I'd only seen him in a small photograph. It was hard not to stare.

He brushed the hair from my forehead and said, "I love you as a blonde. It's like you're a new person."

I smiled, wondering if I looked as pale and dreamy as I felt.

He started the car, and turned and looked me up and down. "You're almost perfect. Now all you need is her shoes."

I put my hand to my mouth. "Oh my God. I completely forgot."

He shook his head. "You're just as forgetful as your sister."

"I'm sorry. I just have a lot on my mind. Mom found out I've been hanging out with you. She's been watching me a like a hawk, and she's so mad she wants to send me away to school."

"Well, we can't let that happen." He pulled out into the street. "I thought we'd get a burger on Speedway, but I guess no dancing tonight."

"Guess not." I hoped he wasn't too disappointed.

We raced down the highway, but when we got to Speedway he slowed down. There were so many signs and neon lights; it was like we were in a giant carnival. I took a tube of lipstick out of my purse, put some on and licked my lips. Tony was right. I was a new person. For the first time ever, I felt alive. As we cruised slowly he'd lean out the open window and sometimes talk to people in other cars, almost as if he wanted them to see I was with him. I felt proud.

When we got to Johnie's, he took my hand. His grip was strong, like everything else about him. As we threaded our way across the crowded parking lot, kids greeted him as if he were famous.

"I can't get any privacy," he said when we sat at a booth inside.

I wasn't hungry, but I ordered a burger and fries. I wished I hadn't already eaten dinner. My burger was so big, I felt sick looking at it. All I could manage was about two bites.

Tony leaned across the table. "I'm going to show you that photo now." He glanced around, acting all secretive.

"Okay," I said.

He reached into his pocket, held it up so only he could see, and slid it across the table to me. As I picked it up, he motioned for me not to wave it around.

There were fingerprints on the glossy surface like it had been touched many times, and the edges were cracked. I imagined Tony studying it, missing her. The light in the restaurant was dim, but I could tell it was Jess. She was sitting on a lounge chair on a beach, wearing her red bikini. Her hair was styled in a flip, she wore sunglasses, and she was smiling, her lips parted slightly to show her white teeth. Her small hand was raised, waving to whoever was taking the picture. It reminded me of how she had looked in the dream I'd had when I'd passed out by our pool, Jess waving in sunglasses, going further and further away.

"So," Tony said, "now do you believe she's in California?"

I looked up at him, the realization that my sister really was in Redondo overwhelming me. "Yes."

He smiled slowly. As he started to put the photo back in his pocket, I asked if I could keep it. He stared at me questioningly. I told him I liked looking at it.

"Okay." His gaze drifted to the window as he handed it back. The parking lot was a jumble of cars and kids. He turned to me. "She was wearing that bathing suit the first time I saw her."

"I know. I was there."

He scratched his chin. "You were," he said, as if just remembering this. "I'll never forget that moment." He paused. "She was the first thing I saw when I shot up out of the water. It was like I was prescient. You know what that means?"

I fidgeted with my napkin, unable to shake the sense he was telling this more to himself than me. "No."

"It means you can see things that are going to happen. In that instant I saw everything between her and me." He made a fist and stared at his knuckles. "Prescience was another gift the water gave me." He turned to me, his eyes as luminous as the flashing blues of a police car. When I looked into them, I could have sworn I saw that part of him was human and part of him, the part that came from the water, was something else. It made everything about me—my string of As in school, my friends, the clothes I liked—all seem stupid and irrelevant. For a second, it was like I didn't exist. I stared down at my perfect lavender nails and the thought came to me that I would like to change my name to Caro. It had a touch of mystery to it. I wanted to tell him, but the words wouldn't leave my lips.

He smiled. "I got the car all tuned up. We should be able to get to Redondo in a day. I'll let Brian know we're coming, and tell him not to tell Jess."

"So when exactly are we going?" I asked cautiously.

He seemed to think on this, and then said, "Saturday night. I've got a couple of things I need to do first."

"Saturday?" I almost choked on a bite of burger.

"I thought we went through this." He sounded mad. "You want to just hang around until your parents send you away."

"No." I tore my napkin into pieces. Out the window, red and white lights distorted in the evening air as cars cruised past. "Saturday is fine."

"I knew you'd come around. It'll be fun. We'll go to the beach, swim, hang out, and you'll convince Jess to come back with us. Before you know it, we'll be sitting here again, all three of us." He looked me in the eye. "When I foresee something will work out, it usually happens."

I looked away. The way he referred to a future beyond California, a time when we'd all be together, reassured me, though at the same time I didn't want to think of Jess being back with Tony.

He touched my hand. "What's wrong? This is what you want, isn't it?"

"It is, but when Jess comes back she'll be with you, not me. I know that sounds selfish, and I'm sorry for that."

He shook his head. "Sweetheart, much as we were something once, now Jess hates the ground I walk on, but you . . . ." He paused, studying me. "You're my girl." He closed his hand around mine, and a sweet wave washed through me. I wanted to laugh and cry at the same time.

When the waitress took our plates away, he put some money on the table and frowned. "I really wanted to see you in those shoes."

"I told you I was sorry," I said.

"I know, but I can still wish it, can't I?" He smiled, leaning his face on his palm. I couldn't stop staring at his lips. "Just bring it next time. When we find your sister, I promise that you and me, we'll go dancing." As he took my hands in his and raised them up like we were already dancing, warm feelings rushed through me.

I let go and glanced at my watch. "I better go."

He cocked his head. "But we haven't even gotten started."

I sighed. "I know, but it's a school night. I have to be home early."

He rubbed his chin with his hand. "You always gotta leave, but I guess we'll have plenty of time alone together soon."

"We will." I tasted burger at the back of my throat.

"Just promise me one thing," he said. I looked up. "Don't breathe a word about this to anyone." His eyes were chilly as the sea on a windy day. He pressed his knees against mine under the table. All the time he'd been Jess's boyfriend, it was like I'd never seen who he really was, but now I did, and he was real as the grass growing out of the dark earth, as an orange dangling from an orange tree, as real as could be.

"I won't tell," I said.

CHAPTER 20

On Thursday before walking to school, I paused in front of my house. Since we'd moved here it had never really felt like home, but now, strangely, it did. I noticed the orange sherbet color of the stucco, rough as sandpaper, and how the hibiscus flowers by the front door matched the red tile roof. It was a nice little house with a lawn that Dad kept green with endless watering, and a single mesquite tree with its own crooked shadow. I stepped back to take it all in. No cars backed out of driveways. No planes zoomed overhead. No one but me was outside. From our street all the way to the desert's yellow emptiness, everything was as silent as a page in a storybook.

My name is Caro, I thought, and I'm going to California with Tony. I took the picture of Jess out of my purse where I'd put it that morning so it would be with me wherever I went. I wanted to show the photo to everyone I saw, the knowledge that Jess was somewhere and that we were going to find her almost too hard to contain, but I knew I couldn't do that. From somewhere far away, a bird sang a lonely song.

In school I said silent goodbyes to everyone. They weren't forever goodbyes. I was coming back, but when I did, nothing would be the same. Everyone would be happy to see Jess, and know it was because of me. My parents would be sorry for saying I couldn't see Tony, and glad I hadn't listened. They would regret everything. I would be a new person.

As I went from class to class, I felt like the ghost of this person I had been, floating around the corridors, my thoughts expanding far beyond this little place that smelled of chalk and disinfectant. And then I thought, what was a ghost anyway but a shadow of something that was, and since we were changing every minute of every day, weren't we all ghosts of ourselves, all of us except for Tony? When he opened his eyes after drowning, it must have been like time stopped as he rose up through all the ghosts of himself into who he really was. I was so lost in these thoughts, I walked right by my locker and had to go back to get my books. As I ran down the nearly empty hall, already late for class, I bumped into a teacher.

"Who are you? Where are you going?" he asked sternly.

"Caro," I said. He gave me a puzzled look and let me go.

In English, May and I didn't speak. Out of the corner of my eye, I glimpsed her writing in her notebook. She was probably writing another stupid poem about not being thin enough.

Mr. Raymond was saying something about our unit on poetry being over when the intercom buzzed. An announcement came on. My stomach lurched as I heard the words, "Will Caroline Galvin please report to Principal Shannon's office?"

May watched me leave with a bemused look, her cheek on her palm. A wave of panic went through me. Had she told the principal something bad about me?

My father was sitting on a chair in the office with a grim expression on his face. I inhaled sharply. Mr. Shannon shuffled some papers around on his desk. I braced myself for him to ask about me and Tony in front of Dad.

"Your dad has come to take you home," was all he said. He didn't sound angry. He seemed like he felt sorry for me. Dad took my hand. I had the sinking feeling that my trip to California was over. I had no idea how he'd found out about it since I hadn't told anyone.

When we got outside he fixed his sad eyes on me. "Caroline, I don't know any other way to say this, so I'm just going to tell you. They found a body."

"No," I said, backing away.

"It's the body of a girl. She was buried in the desert." He rubbed his forehead and sighed. "They don't know if it's Jess, but we have to be prepared for the worst."

"It's not Jess. It can't be." He looked so distressed I couldn't bear it. Not being able to say anything pulled me apart, but I couldn't tell him she was in California. If I told and they sent the police to look for her, Jess might take off. We might never find her. I couldn't let that happen.

Mom was in the living room when we got home. She looked up, her eyes puffy from crying, and reached her arms out to me. I buried myself in them. "Caroline," she said through tears. When she let me go, the look on her face was as if she was steeling herself for the end of the world.

"They don't know if it's Jess," she said.

"I'm sure it isn't." I put my hand on my purse with the photo safely tucked inside.

"We can only hope so." Dad took Mom's hand. "The police had an anonymous tip. They're still trying to trace it."

"Dicky's staying at Betty Beckham's until things are sorted out here. She's a saint," Mom said. I hadn't even noticed that Dicky wasn't around. Everyone forgot about him lately. We were all too busy thinking about Jess.

I went over to the window. The new yellow curtains were tied back, revealing another beautiful sunny day. It was probably sunny in Redondo as well. I pictured Jess splashing in the surf, with no idea that Mom and Dad were sitting here imagining the worst. This was going to be the longest day of my life. I knew that already. We sat in silence, staring at each other like statues in a museum. Then Mom said she was going to make some coffee, and I went up to my room.

I sat down on my bed and took the picture out of my purse, put my finger on my sister's face and thought, everyone thinks you're dead but you aren't. The picture was blurry, but that didn't matter. I didn't need a picture to remember the way Jess's green eyes stared right through me, to see her jiggling her foot, drumming her nails on the table, fidgeting, turning from whatever was in front of her so as not to miss the next great thing. A picture could never capture someone like Jess. She was never still.

I put my head in my hands and thought, Jess, please stay in Redondo until I get there. Don't take off. Don't do that to me. There was no answer. I put the photo back in my purse and then did this thing I hadn't done in years—I knelt down beside the bed, my knees pressing into the stiff, pink carpet, and prayed.

I'm sorry, God, for smoking pot, I said in my mind. I'm sorry for kissing Tony when Jess was missing, and liking it. I'm sorry for caring more about my friends than looking for her. I'm sorry for all of this, and I'll give everything up if you'll just make her stay in one place long enough for me to find her.

When I was finished, I got Jess's pretty white shoe out of the closet. Soon I would be dancing. Soon we'd all be dancing. I held the shoe close to my chest and rose on my tiptoes like a ballerina, the knowledge of California dancing within me. I heard a tap on my door. I hurriedly tossed the shoe back in the closet. Mom leaned in, her face pale and haggard.

She fingered the doorframe hesitantly. "I wanted to make sure you were okay."

"I'm fine." I gave her a dismissive glance, angry with her for intruding on my private moment of hope.

"Well if you need anything . . . ." She kept staring at me.

"Really, Mom, I'm okay."

"Good." She backed away, her gaze still clinging to me.

As she softly clicked the door shut, a terrible thought occurred to me. If things didn't get figured out soon, I might not be able to go California. There would be no triumphant finding of Jess, because my parents would never let me out of their sight. Things would keep going on the way they were, everyone paralyzed by grief over something that hadn't actually happened. How I wished I could tell them Jess was in California, and not buried in the desert. I tore a tiny piece of dry skin off my lip and flicked it on to the rug. Then I flopped down on my bed, grabbed the pink spread, and twisted it up in my hands. Tears stung my eyes. In her own strange way, Jess had showed me a way out into the world. Her restless energy carried her to places I couldn't imagine going to. She did all the wrong things I never dared to do. Without her to lead me I might never get out of here.

We didn't hear anything that day or the next. No one could say a word to Mom without her bursting out crying. When she wasn't crying, she was looking at Dad as if he'd ruined her life. On Saturday morning, she made pancakes for breakfast though no one wanted to eat. I helped her clean up while Dad sat at the table reading the paper. Each time he'd rustle the pages, she would flinch.

When he came over and asked for more coffee, she whirled around and said, "What is wrong with you?"

Dad stepped back. "Nothing. My coffee's cold." He refilled his cup. I held my breath.

As he sat back down, Mom said, "No, really, what is wrong with you?"

He looked at her over the rim of his mug. "What are you talking about?"

I wiped a glass with a dishcloth, pretending not to hear.

"I don't understand how you can keep acting like everything is okay. Our daughter is probably dead and you sip your coffee like it's any other day."

"Frances." He used a formal tone. "You know that isn't true. I'm as upset as you are."

Mom shook her head. "No, you aren't. You have your scotch and your coffee and your golf and your paper and nothing ever gets to you. You just . . . ." She flung her hands up. "Keep going. I wish I could do that. I wish all these years, whenever we had a problem with Jess, I could just have downed another scotch and forgotten about it."

I stared at the glass in my hand, afraid to move.

Dad pushed his chair back. "I'm not going to listen to this anymore."

"Go on then. Go wherever it is you're going to go, because I don't care anymore, not about you, not about any of this." She glared at him. "And now I have to plan my daughter's funeral, because no one else is going to do it." She gave Dad a miserable glance.

The glass slipped through my fingers and shattered.

"I'm sorry. I'm sorry." I crouched down to pick up the pieces.

"Stop. You'll cut yourself," Mom said. She swept the broken glass into the dustpan with such fury it was as if she hated it. When she was through, she turned to us, tears running down her cheeks.

Dad grabbed her by the shoulders. As he pulled her to him, she pounded his chest with her fists. "I can't do this," she repeated through sobs.

Before I knew what I was saying the words, "You don't need to worry, she's okay," spilled out of my mouth.

Mom turned to me with agonizing slowness. "No, she isn't. Dear God, no, she isn't. Can't anyone face this?"

I looked down at my hand. A tiny bubble of blood had formed on a cut on my finger. I wrapped my other hand around it tight so it wouldn't hurt too much.

For the rest of the day, I waited for the police to call and say it wasn't Jess. But hours passed and no one called. I paced from one end of the room to the other, unable to sit still. It was Saturday. Tony and I were leaving for California that night. It was going to be hard to leave, but I had to. After dinner I threw a bathing suit, my black-and-white dress, shorts, and some jeans into a black canvas bag printed with giant daisies, feeling nauseated as I did it.

It was seven thirty, only half an hour until I was supposed to meet Tony. All I needed to do was tell my parents I was going to study with Billy. They would be glad to get me out of the house so they could dwell on their misery without me around. But I couldn't lie to Mom and run off to California with things the way they were. She would go out of her mind with worry. I wished Tony would call and persuade me. I needed to hear him say that the most important thing was finding Jess, that everyone would understand once we brought her back, that I needed to be brave. But he didn't call.

I was ready to give up on going when I had an idea. I sat down at my desk, tore a page out of my notebook and wrote:

Dear Mom and Dad,

Don't worry. I'm safe and on my way to find Jess. I will be back with her very soon!

I love you,

Caroline

I taped it to Jess's mirror. They'd never miss it there. Then I grabbed my bag and went down to the living room. Mom and Dad were having a drink and watching TV.

I was trying to summon the courage to tell them I was going out when Dad patted the cushion next to him and said, "Come on over, kitten. Sit with us."

Reluctantly, I sat down between them. They were watching some comedy show. Canned laughter filled the air. Mom gave her skirt a tug so I was no longer sitting on it, and took a sip of her gin and tonic. I glanced anxiously at my watch. It was close to eight o'clock.

I cleared my throat when the commercial came on. "I was thinking . . . ."

Dad ruffled my hair. "I'm so glad you're here." He looked at Mom. "Aren't you, Frances?"

A smile soft as the sun through clouds appeared on her face. "I am," she said. She took my hand, and touched my lavender nails with unexpected affection. As her cool fingers slipped away, it was like they left threads that held on to me. The TV droned on and on.

I went over to the window. Stars twinkled above this world that was as closed in as a snow globe. After a minute or so, Tony's gold car cruised slowly by. I held my breath as its red taillights vanished around the corner.

Make your excuse and leave, I thought, do it now, but I lingered, my hand pressed on the glass, watching. And then the phone rang. Dad and Mom looked at each other. It rang again. I didn't think either of them could bring themselves to answer it, but finally Dad went in the kitchen and got it.

He came back in after a few minutes with a look of profound relief on his face. "That was the police," he announced. "It wasn't Jess."

"Thank the Lord." Mom squeezed her eyes shut for a second. Then we all hugged. I wanted to squirm out of her arms and rush out the door, but I didn't.

"It's another girl, and that *is* a tragedy, but it's not our Jess," she went on triumphantly. "The only news that would be better is finding out where she is and having her come home."

I thought of Tony, still waiting for me around the corner, I hoped. "Mom," I started to say.

She beamed. "Let's do something to celebrate. Caroline, how about if I make s'mores?"

"Okay." There was nothing I wanted to do less than eat a bunch of chocolate and marshmallow, but she was staring at me with such intensity I couldn't say no.

Dad looked up with an idiotic grin. "I'll have s'more of this scotch."

She made a face at him and dashed into the kitchen. I heard drawers opening and closing. I picked up my bag and edged my way over to the door.

Dad raised his eyebrows. "Where are you going?"

"I'm studying with Billy again." I brushed a strand of hair from my mouth.

He smiled. "No s'mores?"

"Maybe later." I bounced on my heels, feeling as if I was about to jump off the high dive into cold water.

"Study hard." Dad waved pathetically. Once outside, I ran down the street as fast as I could, my bag banging against my leg. My breath burned in my throat. When I rounded the corner his car was gone. As I stared in disbelief at the blank spot where it must have been, I wanted to cry. I imagined him waiting for me, then gunning the engine and taking off in disgust. I'd let him down.

I walked slowly back to the house. Dad was still exactly where I'd left him. "That was fast," he said.

"He didn't want to study." I sank back down on the sofa, knowing I'd missed my big chance, and, as always, it was my fault. I tried to watch the show on TV, but its gaiety disturbed me. I wondered if Tony was feeling the same thing I was now—as if there really was no escape.

Dad rubbed his eyes. "This has been a long few days. I'm so relieved."

"Me too." I stood up. There was something I wanted to ask though I wasn't sure I should. I cleared my throat. "Do they know who the girl in the desert was?"

"That poor little girl named Geraldine Keanen," he said.

The blood rushed from my face.

"Are you all right?" he asked.

As I told him I was just tired, I saw Mom standing in the hall with a tray of s'mores. "Geraldine?" She looked at Dad. He nodded.

They stared at each other a moment, and then she put the tray down on the coffee table. "Why don't you have a s'more?" she said to me.

"I'm not really hungry, Mom."

Dad plucked one off the tray and took a bite. "Aren't you having one?" he asked her.

"No." She stared at me. "I don't understand why we can't be happy, even for a minute."

"But these are great, hon," Dad said with a weak smile.

"You have chocolate on your mouth." She gave him a disdainful glance, and he began frantically wiping his lips with a napkin.

I tore the note off the mirror and threw it away. As I sat on my bed, I thought about what Edie had said about the body in the desert, and the terrible thing she claimed Tony had done. Did she even know Geraldine? Tony said that Edie lied. Everyone did. She could have made everything up, maybe even believed it in her crazy way, and then been right by accident. The fact that they'd found Geraldine in the desert was just a strange coincidence, the same way as when you dream about a blue bottle and see one exactly like it in a store window the next day; it means nothing. At Tony's party, I'd seen Jess in another world in the green folds of my dress. The man in *The Doors of Perception* had gotten lost staring at the folds of his pants when he was tripping on mescaline. But that was just a strange coincidence, too. The world was full of coincidences once you started to notice. Still, cold anxiety radiated through me. I thought of what May and Sheila had said weeks ago about Geraldine. How had they known that she was murdered? And I remembered seeing Geraldine's pale and depressing mother at The Flying Saucer restaurant. The police were probably calling her right this minute, giving her the news my parents had been dreading.

If the phone had rung an hour earlier, I'd be on my way to California with Tony now, not troubled by any of this. I thought of the tender way he had touched me, the drifting-petal sadness in his blue eyes, how we were going to find Jess together. This was more important than the crazy things Edie had said, and, if I had to admit it, more important than Geraldine. Tony would probably be so mad at me for not showing up; he might never speak to me again. But if what Edie said was true, I could never speak to *him* again.

Early Sunday morning, the Beckhams' car pulled up in front of our house. I stood outside with Mom and watched Dicky come running toward us. He practically knocked her down, he was so excited to see her. As she hugged him, she looked over his head at Ron getting out of the car, wearing a pink shirt. He grinned at her. She let Dicky go.

"Take your brother inside," she said to me.

I held Dicky's hand, unable to move, as she walked toward him.

Ron said, "So how's everything?"

"Okay." She shrugged. "Except for . . . you know . . . ."

They leaned close, saying something I couldn't hear. They stared at each other a little too long, and then Ron got back in the car. After he drove away she turned to me, her face oddly radiant. My mother was a different person when she was with Ron. I wasn't sure exactly how, but she was. It was like she wasn't my mother.

CHAPTER 21

I didn't hear from Tony for the rest of the weekend. On Monday, there were two police cars parked outside the school. I walked past them, worried that somehow they knew what Edie had told me, and were looking for me. I became even more nervous in homeroom when I learned they were going to talk to kids about Geraldine. Though I knew nothing about her, I almost had a nervous breakdown when my name was called. I'd never had detention, never even had to stay after school. And now, though I hadn't done anything wrong, I felt like I had.

I made my lonely walk down the hall, and pushed open the door to the office with its square of frosted glass. May and Sheila were sitting on a bench along one wall. May slid over to make room. I sat down next to them. They didn't look happy to see me. I hadn't spoken to either of them since I'd said that thing about Mom and Ron.

May pulled a small white compact from her purse, stared at her perfect face in the round mirror, and lightly brushed her cheeks with the pressed powder. She turned to Sheila. "I hate that my skin is so blotchy."

Sheila looked at her adoringly. "You're kidding. Your skin is perfect."

I leaned back and drummed my fingers on the bench. May put her compact back in her purse, careful not to let her eyes meet mine. A tortoiseshell comb fell out. "Geez." She reached under the bench for it.

The skinny secretary sitting across from us said, "Quiet, girls." Sheila smirked at May.

The door to the principal's office opened and Debbie Frank stepped out. She walked past us with her head held high, pausing only to tap the arm of the bench next to me.

When she was gone, Sheila leaned toward May and whispered, "I can't believe they have us here with someone like her. It's not like we know anything."

May whispered back, "I know."

"I never even met Geraldine," I said. Neither of them said a word. Apparently they'd forgotten they were the ones who'd told me the rumors about her. It was strange how you could be sitting right next to two people who you once thought were your friends and feel so far away from them, and not even care.

I fidgeted with the ruby-slipper keychain I'd attached to the zipper of my purse. It looked like something a kid would have. Why hadn't I noticed this before? I wet my finger and rubbed some dust off my black patent leather shoes that I loved so much. They didn't look new anymore.

The secretary touched the glittering bird pin on her lapel. The principal leaned out of his office and said, "Caroline Galvin."

As I stood up, May raised her narrow eyes just enough to show me a flicker of interest.

Mr. Shannon was sitting in his reclining chair, his hands folded on his stomach, a weary expression on his face. He nodded toward a small chair on the other side of his desk where I suspected kids sat when they were in trouble. As I sat down, I gave my jean skirt a tug so it wouldn't ride up.

Officer Barnes was sitting next to me. When he glanced at me with his husky dog eyes, I smiled in spite of myself, grateful to see a familiar face.

He leaned forward. "Caroline, I'm sorry I'm not here with news of your sister, but I want to let you know I've made it my personal mission to find her, and I will."

"Thank you," I said softly.

"Do you know why we're talking to you today?" I shook my head. He went on, "We have reason to believe some of the kids in this school know something about what happened to Geraldine Keanen. They may even know something about what happened to your sister." He rocked back in his chair. "Does that surprise you?"

"Yes." I could barely speak.

"It's hard to understand how kids could know things that might help and not tell anyone."

"It is." I looked up at the tiny transom window above the door, wondering if I could squeeze through it.

He cleared his throat. "Geraldine was a good student, like you." He glanced at Mr. Shannon and back at me. "I believe she liked science. Do you like science?" His tone was so strangely kind.

"I like English better than science, but I'm interested in the stars."

Mr. Shannon cleared his throat. "Geraldine was interested in the ocean. She won the science fair two years ago." He lowered his eyes. "A great loss."

Officer Barnes shook his head. "It is a tragic loss when a smart young girl with so much ahead of her dies needlessly."

I crossed my legs one way and then the other, wishing he'd stop talking about dying.

"Her mother is devastated. You must know how that feels. Your mother is devastated, too, but at least there is still hope for finding Jess. All that's left for Geraldine's mother is finding out what really happened to her daughter and making sure whoever did it never does something like that again." His light eyes lingered on me. He went on, "A nice girl like you would tell if you knew something that would help her, wouldn't you?"

"I would." I wondered why he was saying these things to me when I'd never even met Geraldine. I thought of the photo of Jess in my purse, like a good-luck charm, wishing I could tell him about it, knowing I couldn't.

His expression became stern. "Did you know Tony Santoro dated Geraldine?"

"No." My breath escaped from me.

"Does that surprise you?"

"It does." I glanced at the door, wanting this to be over.

"Geraldine's mother said Geraldine broke up with him and he didn't take it well. He was angry. He threatened her. Of course, we can't prove that. At the time, we couldn't even prove they were dating. It was puzzling. No one except her mother seemed to know."

"I didn't know, either." I thought of the way her mother looked at me in the restaurant. Why would she lie about Tony? But nobody else thought they were dating. May and Sheila hadn't even mentioned that.

"Are you sure?" When I didn't answer, he edged closer to me. "Caroline, we know you've been hanging around with Tony."

How did he know this? I tried to look away, but it was like his eyes were pinning me to the spot. I worried they were special, all-seeing eyes, and he knew I'd kissed Tony. The thought of what he might tell my parents made me uneasy. I felt my resolve crumbling.

Careful not to look away, I said, "I've only been hanging around with him because he said he'd help me find my sister."

He shook his head as if I'd said the most awful thing. "I'm the one who can help you find your sister. Tony isn't. No matter how nice he seems, Tony's a dangerous guy. You need to stay away from him. He and his friends are bad kids, but I know you're not like them."

I glanced up at a framed photo of the high-school football team on the wall. The thought, I'm a ghost of myself, slipped through my mind, making me nervous. Everything was sliding away, impossible to grasp as egg white. It would be so easy to tell him everything, to rely on him to find Jess. But he hadn't found her yet. Maybe he never would. And I was so close to finding her. "I don't hang around with him anymore."

"Good." He paused. "Now, I want you to think hard. Did Tony say anything about Geraldine when you were with him? It can be the smallest thing."

"I don't remember anything." The terrible thing Edie had said worked its way into my thoughts, but I pushed it away. I worried it was a crime not to tell him, but if I told him, they would arrest Tony, and my chance of going to California and finding Jess would be ruined. I folded my arms across my chest, as if by doing this I could keep myself from falling apart.

He leaned so close I could see the dark hairs on the backs of his hands, his thick-ridged nails. "We believe the anonymous caller might have been a friend of Tony's. Is there anyone you can think of who might have made that call?"

I inhaled sharply. It was like he already knew. I should have said something about Edie right away. Now I was a liar, too. The silence in the room pulsed in my ears. I looked up at the spider web of cracks in the ceiling, wishing it would come crashing down and rescue me from this conversation. "I really can't think of anyone right now." I tried to appear calm.

He shook his head. "That's too bad. It would be helpful to be able to talk to him some more."

For a second I wasn't sure I'd heard right. Him? A wave of relief went through me. Dear God, thank you, I thought, as I said, "I wish I could help you."

We sat there a moment, the three of us, the room so warm I thought I might have a fever. The sun glared on the dusty windows. I looked at the clock, hoping he'd let me go. I'd already missed most of my first class.

"Caroline," Officer Barnes said, almost as if my name were a source of wonder. "Did you ever see Tony hurt your sister?"

I rubbed my hands on my thighs. "No."

"You never saw him strike her?"

"No," I said. There were times, of course, that could give you pause. There was the fight on the phone when we got back from California, his voice so loud I could hear it coming through the receiver Jess held to her ear. Once I'd seen a purple bruise on Tony's arm, and Jess had confided in me almost triumphantly that it was from when he fought a boy because of her. I'd seen all of these things, but I'd never seen him hurt her. I pressed myself against the back of my chair. "Why are you asking me this?"

He smiled sadly. "Because I have to." He went on, "Did your sister ever mention Geraldine?"

"No." I was glad not to have to lie. She had never mentioned Geraldine. I doubted they knew each other, but like everyone else, he was suspicious of Jess. No one ever suspected the good kids, even when they were mean, even when they were the ones who lied.

"Did anyone else ever mention Geraldine to you?" He swiveled his chair to face me.

I bit the inside of my cheek so hard it hurt. It was like he was going to pull the word "Edie" right out of my mouth. I couldn't let that happen. "Some of my friends talked about her once."

"Which friends, Caroline?"

My heart thundered in my chest. There was no turning back. "May and Sheila said something."

Officer Barnes licked the tip of his pencil. "May and Sheila?"

Mr. Shannon nodded toward the door. "They're waiting outside."

Officer Barnes wrote something down. "Do you remember what they said?"

I was sorry I'd brought this up. If I told him that they'd said Geraldine was murdered, he'd think Tony had something to do with it. Everyone always blamed him. "It was a while ago." I twirled a strand of hair around my finger. "They were just talking about rumors." I sucked in my breath. "That kids were spreading about Geraldine."

He sat up straighter. "What rumors?"

I chipped some lavender polish off a nail. "Some kids say they saw her ghost in the desert."

He frowned. "Her ghost?"

"Yeah, you know how kids talk." I tried to look confident.

He took a card exactly like the one he'd given me weeks ago out of his pocket and said, "If you remember anything else, please call me. I want to help you."

Then the principal told me it was okay to go. As I closed my hand around the brass doorknob, Office Barnes said, "Caroline." I turned. A tremor of fear ran through me. He spoke in a calm voice. "Boys like Tony don't change. Chances are if he had trouble with the breakup with Geraldine, he might have had the same kind of trouble with your sister."

I stared at him. "They didn't break up."

He went on as if he hadn't heard me. "And he might have the same sort of trouble with you—I mean, hypothetically."

My cheeks became hot and red as I pushed the door open. May and Sheila glanced up at me. I rushed past as if I hadn't seen them.

CHAPTER 22

For the rest of that day I jumped every time a bell rang, worried that I'd be called back to the office. Kids gossiped about Geraldine in the halls as if she were nothing more than an exciting distraction. It was easy for them to talk about her. They didn't have a sister who was missing. When I was leaving school, I saw Sheila and May standing on the gym steps. Please don't see me, I thought, but they motioned me over.

Sheila looked me up and down. "So?"

I shifted my weight from foot to foot. "What?"

"Why did you tell the cop what we said about Geraldine?"

I glanced over my shoulder. "He asked me. What did you want me to do? Lie? What I said wasn't that bad. I only told him about the ghost."

Sheila frowned. "Except both of us had told him we didn't even know who Geraldine was, so then when he told us what you said, it was super embarrassing."

"I was mortified," May said softly. She reeked of cigarettes. "Linda told us not to tell. You weren't supposed to either." She leaned toward me. "You never ever tell the police more than they need to know. You could get someone in trouble."

I looked up at her. "Like who?"

"I don't know." She squished her hands together. "Like us. The police might think we lied, and talk to our parents."

I stared at the pathetic blades of grass beneath my feet. "I'm sorry about that, but I need to find Jess. I had to tell him what I knew."

"I get it." May gave me a hard look. "Really, I do."

"So do you think they found out anything from any of the other kids?" I asked.

"About what?" May said.

"About Geraldine," I said.

May glanced at Sheila. "I don't know, but *we* didn't say anything else. Maybe you should ask Tony about her, seeing as he's your boyfriend."

I felt an odd mix of thrill and terror. "He's not my boyfriend."

"Glad to hear that." May smoothed her hair and smiled hesitantly. "I read in the newspaper all they found was her bones."

I shuddered. Bones.

Sheila leaned so close I could see the pale freckles on her cheeks. She said in a loud whisper, "Some kids are saying there was still some skin sticking to her bones like leather, kind of like a mummy." I tried to swallow, but I couldn't.

"I wonder if she was wearing anything," May whispered. "Or if she was naked?"

Sheila widened her eyes. "They found a scrap of her dress." She went on, "I heard the grave was really close to the drinking spot."

"You mean the place in the desert where the kids party?" I felt like I was about to throw up.

She nodded. "Imagine having a beer and not knowing she was buried right next to you."

May shook her head. "I didn't think Geraldine even went to those parties. She didn't fit in with those kids. They thought she was kind of a freak." She stared straight at me and added, "She didn't know enough about people to see when someone might hurt her."

"Why are you telling me this?" I said. "Is there something else I should know?"

"No." May's eyes flicked away. "It's just stuff kids are talking about. You must have heard it. Everyone has." She twisted the silver ring on her finger. "We're just happy it wasn't Jess."

It was so hot I thought I might melt as I stood there with them. Nothing moved. No one said anything. I had a hunch they were still keeping things from me, but why? Maybe it was just all rumors, but I hadn't heard them. May had said I should ask Tony about Geraldine. Had Officer Barnes told her the same thing about Tony dating her that he'd told me? Or did she know something else? Finally I said, "I didn't even know Geraldine and I feel bad," and it was strange because as I said this, for the first time I did feel bad for her. I'd never known anyone who'd died except for my grandfather, but that wasn't the same. A hot wind brushed our faces with sand. It had a stale smell like it came from some place old and far away. We were silent, the terribleness of what had happened to Geraldine touching us, and bringing us together in the strange way that tragic things do.

May finally smiled and said, "Want to come over my house with Sheila? We're going to watch TV and pretend to do homework."

She acted like we could be friends again without ever having talked about the mean things she'd done, or what she could still be hiding from me. "I have to go home. My mom needs me."

They looked at me sadly and walked in one direction while I went in the other. Sweat stung my eyes. A fine layer of dust clung to my clothes. In the distance, the white sky met the horizon as if sealing me shut in this place forever. I felt like I was being buried. It was hard to take another step, but I pushed myself forward. A car approached. I didn't turn until it was so close I could see the film of dirt on the gold door.

Tony leaned out the window. "Get in. I'll give you a ride."
I wouldn't look at him. He followed me slowly in the car as I
walked, my nerves spiraling out of control.

"Come on, Caroline, talk to me," he said. "I'm not mad at
you for standing me up Saturday night, if that's what you think."

I turned. My reflection shimmered like a mirage in his
mirrored sunglasses. I supposed I owed him an explanation.
"After what happened with Geraldine, my parents wouldn't let
me out of their sight. And they certainly wouldn't let me hang
out with you."

"Sounds like I'm in the doghouse." He cocked his head.

"I guess." My thin cotton shirt was sticking to my back.

"I don't suppose you'd want to get in and talk about it." His
voice was soft as velvet.

"I don't think I should."

"Caroline," he said, "a few days ago you were going with me
to find your sister and now you won't even talk to me. What's
going on?"

"Nothing." I stared down at my dusty shoes.

"I'm beginning to wonder if you even want to find Jess."

I gave him an agonized glance. I thought about the things
Officer Barnes had said about him, and all my doubts. But I
couldn't stop looking for Jess when we were so close. It was like I
was being torn in two. "I still want to find her."

"So get in. If something's wrong, for Christ's sake, give me a
chance to explain." He paused. "I thought you wanted to go on
the road with me—to be free. Jess always wanted to be free."

I opened the door as if in a dream.

As I drew it shut, May and Sheila stopped a few blocks away,
turned and stared at me in shock. Let them stare, I thought. Tony
pushed his sunglasses on top of his head and rubbed his eyes. His
skin glistened with sweat. I could smell the sharp tang of it.

He leaned forward. "So how did your parents find out about me?"

I bit down on my lip. "May told them."

"May, what a surprise." He smiled.

"She and Sheila said some really sick things about Geraldine too." The throw-up feeling was returning but I went on, "They said she was mummified."

"They said that? That is sick." He looked down the street to the place where they just were. I shifted in my seat. The vinyl was burning the backs of my thighs. He walked his fingers over to mine. "We're still good, right?"

I tried to speak, but no words came out. The way he was looking at me with such trust, not even aware that the whole world was against him, broke my heart. "A policeman came to my school. He asked me about Geraldine. And he knew I was hanging out with you. He said you were a bad person." I looked away.

He leaned back. "God, will these people ever leave me alone?" He stared at the dirt-spattered windshield. "I hope this isn't the end of us." He sounded already resigned to his fate.

"He told me to stay away from you." I opened my purse, took out my compact and looked into the mirror. I'd felt so happy and hopeful when Tony and I were together. Everything was so confusing. Trying to hold back tears, I blotted the sweat from my nose with the puff. A single teardrop stained the pink powder.

He brushed my tears away with his thumb. "Do I really seem like a bad person to you?"

"No." His hand was warm against my cheek. "You seem like the only one who cares about finding my sister."

He shook his head as if the world was the sorriest place. "I do. More than anyone knows." I followed his gaze to the disappearing line where the sky met the earth. I knew how awful he felt. He turned slowly back to me. "What did he ask you about Geraldine?"

I looked down at my chipped nails. "Nothing, really."

"Nothing?"

I hesitated, still staring at my nails. I needed to find out about this. "He asked if I knew she was your girlfriend and that she broke up with you."

He slammed his fist so hard against the dash that it left a small hollow in the plastic. "I hate the way people lie."

I spoke softly, not wanting to get him more riled up. "She wasn't your girlfriend?"

"No. And she certainly didn't break up with me." He hit the dash again.

"Stop, you'll hurt yourself." I fiddled with the keychain on my purse. Red glitter came off on my hands. "Do you have any idea who might have called the police about her?"

"Nope. But must have been someone with a guilty conscience." He paused. "Or someone out to get me. I'm so sick of everyone blaming me for everything. I bet you believed everything the police told you." He glared at me. "I know what you're thinking, but I swear to God I had nothing to do with what happened to Geraldine."

"Why should I believe you?" I had to say it.

"Because this is me. Tony. The guy who's going to help you find your sister." He started the car. His silence as he drove made me feel so alone. I'd said what I was supposed to say, but it went against everything I felt. Officer Barnes was just like my parents, and Ron and Joe, all the clueless adults who said they'd find my sister and hadn't.

Finally I said, "Please don't be mad at me. I don't believe any of the bad things people are saying."

He glanced at me out of the corner of his eye. "Are we still going to California?" My relief mixed with worry. "Brian told me Jess is getting restless. He doesn't think she'll stick around much longer. We have to leave Friday."

"Friday?" I looked out the window. Sprinklers were going round and round in all the yards. I remembered riding on a carousel with Jess when I was a little girl. I'd held on to the neck of the plaster horse as if for dear life, afraid to reach out for the brass ring, but now I wished I could reach out the window and grab the whole world and take it with me.

"If you don't want to go, just tell me," he said. "I'll go myself."

"I want to go. It's not that." I paused. "It's just everything." My feelings were pulling me in all different directions. To walk away would be to give up like everyone else, but I couldn't ignore the doubts that filled me.

"You know what I think?" His voice grew quieter. "Let's have a good time first, and then we'll talk about finding Jess."

"What do you mean?"

He pulled up to the curb a block from my house and said, "I think you need to go dancing."

I turned to him, surprised.

Those lips that had kissed mine smiled. "Think up a good excuse for your mom, 'cause I'm picking you up tomorrow night at seven. We'll have dinner first, just the two of us." He stroked my hand.

I nodded, hoping it would be as easy as he made it sound. And then he leaned over and kissed me. His mouth on mine was delicious and sad at the same time. It was like our edges blurred and for a split second we stepped into a new world—the world of us. He sat back and sighed.

A smile crossed my face. "I forgot to tell you something."

He cocked his head. "What? Is your policeman friend following us?"

I laughed. "No. I've changed my name to Caro."

"Caro?" His eyes widened. "Well, Caro, wear your prettiest dress tomorrow night." He paused. "And remember to bring that white shoe. I can't wait to see you in them. We'll dance the night away." As I was opening the door he touched my arm. "I know I haven't always been the best person, but I appreciate that you're standing by me." He pulled me close and kissed me again. I would have liked to have stayed in his arms forever, but I worried someone might walk by and see us.

"I better get home," I said.

He pressed his palm against mine. "Caro," he said, "I wish I never had to let you go."

We ate dessert in the living room that night so we could watch the news, all of us anxious to hear what they said about Geraldine. Dessert was vanilla pudding with strawberries, one of my favorites. When the story about Geraldine came on, Dad placed his cigarette on the edge of his ashtray. Dicky looked up from crashing his toy airplanes into each other. The newscaster spoke in front of a photo of Geraldine. She looked like a sweeter version of Jess, her shoulder-length blonde hair falling in soft waves. I looked down at the untouched skin of my pudding, the strawberries staining it pink. Mom fiddled with the diamond stud in her ear. The newscaster said that the police had questioned some of Geraldine's friends, including Debbie Frank, Moose (his real name was Mike Saunders), and Tony Santoro. At the mention of Tony's name, I tensed. I waited for my parents to say that Officer Barnes had told them I was hanging around with him, but they were too lost in their own worlds to say anything. Jess was the one who was missing, but it was as if we were all spinning away from each other.

The screen filled with a scene of the desert at night. A blurry white glow from a flashlight shone on something in a ditch in the sand. It was hard to tell exactly what it was. I leaned forward, not sure I wanted to see it. The newscaster talked about how scraps of her clothing were used to identify her. I squinted. Was that white smudge in the darkness a bone? I hated that I was made of bones. I sucked on my fist. When they cut to commercial, I breathed a sigh of relief. They hadn't mentioned me or Jess.

"Her poor mother." Mom smoothed her skirt. I ate a bite of pudding.

Dad went over to the window and pressed his hands on the glass as he looked out. "That bastard," he said. "If he did anything to that poor little girl or . . . ."

"Please stop." She sank back on the couch. "We all know you're not going to do anything."

He turned around slowly, took a last puff of his cigarette and said, "I'm going out for a while."

"Jack, don't, I'm sorry," she said. He slammed the door behind him.

She picked up our dessert dishes in her efficient, automatic way and took them into the kitchen. I went over to the window. As I watched Dad's car pull out of the driveway, I fingered the yellow curtains she'd made, longing for the time when her biggest problem was redecorating. After a while I went to get another pudding. Mom still always made five.

The dishes were neatly stacked in the dish drainer. A lemony scent filled the air. Mom had cleaned as ceaselessly as on any other night. I picked up the newspaper from the table. There was an article about Geraldine on the front page. I read it, eager for every detail. When asked if Geraldine was dating Tony when she disappeared, her mom had said she was dating another boy, but it was possible she'd gone to see Tony that night. She was a sweet girl. She cared about everyone. I should have stopped right there. In the next paragraph, her mother said Geraldine had left the house wearing a blue dress and new white ankle strap shoes that she'd picked out from the Sears catalogue. She'd been so excited about them, it made no sense she wasn't wearing them when they found her. I put down the newspaper.

The air conditioning in the kitchen was turned up so high it gave me goose bumps. I wrapped my arms around myself, recalling the creamy firmness of Tony's arms as he held me, the way he smelled of cologne, cigarettes, and sweat—a scent prettier than any flowers. But even this memory could not keep the cold from spreading through me.

I hurried upstairs. My fingers trembled as I opened the closet door and groped in the darkness. My hand shook as I held it up; the shoe white as snow, white as marble, white as Tony's mask face when he played with his band. On the inside of it, below the ankle strap, written in tiny gold cursive letters, was the word "Sears." Mom never bought us anything from Sears. I squeezed my eyes shut, wishing I could make the shoe disappear.

CHAPTER 23

It's just a shoe, I told myself as I got ready to go out with Tony, but the awful thoughts kept coming. I'd considered many reasons why my sister had run away—pursuing her dreams, a fight with Tony, chasing Arnie. I still didn't have an answer, but I worried the real reason was far worse, and that it had to do with Geraldine. I couldn't imagine going out at all, let alone for dinner and dancing, but I couldn't just stay home and wait patiently while things went on the same as ever. I couldn't be that person anymore.

I took care getting ready. I wore my new white dress with the colored squares and my black patent leather shoes. I put on filigree earrings that looked like golden snowflakes, and painted my nails black with a small white daisy on each one. I sprayed perfume on my wrists and behind my ears. I put on a little too much.

I took the photo of Jess out of my purse. She looked happy, sitting on the sand in her red bathing suit, waving her pale hand, a carefree smile on her face. The water behind her was the same silver-blue as the ocean in Boston, sailboats skimming along the horizon. It was comforting that the faraway place where she was now looked so much like beaches back home, and that the Jess in the picture looked just like the Jess I'd always known, not the Jess who had Geraldine's shoe. The very idea of touching it made me ill. I couldn't bring it with me. I hoped when I explained this to Tony that he would understand, and that he would know why Jess had it. I prayed what he said would put my mind at ease.

I put the photo on her bureau and looked in the mirror. I'd ironed my blonde hair and parted it on the side so it hid half my face. I outlined my eyes with black and used white eye shadow. When I lifted my lids, there they were—my tiger eyes. I am dark water flowing into the now, I thought. I am Caro. I looked detached and cool, though I was a jittering jangling mess of nerves.

I pushed the kitchen door open. Mom was on the phone, her back turned to me, a lit cigarette in her hand. Dicky sat at the table, engrossed in his dinner of fried hot dogs and beans.

"He took off last night like he always does. He didn't get home until after midnight," I heard her say. I held myself still. Her hand went to her mouth, smoke drifting up around her. "When they showed that grave on the news, it tore me apart. And what does he do? He leaves." There was more smoke. "And tonight, he's not even home for dinner. No call. Nothing. He always takes off when I need him." She cupped her hand around her mouth. "No, you're right. I don't need him. Not anymore."

I coughed and she turned. "Excuse me, I have to go." She hung up the phone. "Caroline." She smiled hesitantly, spots of color on her cheeks.

"I was talking to Betty," she said. "She's such a good listener." She rubbed her cigarette out in a silver ashtray on the table. "Do you want a hot dog?"

"Actually, I'm going to Sheila's tonight for pizza. Okay?"

"That's fine, hon." She hadn't even noticed I'd changed out of my school clothes. She sat down at the table with Dicky. "Your dad must be working late again."

"I'm sure he'll be home soon." I forced a smile.

"With him, I'm not sure about anything." She took a sip of her gin and tonic.

I looked away, not wanting to talk to her about Dad. I tugged on the hem of my dress, trying to smooth it out. Though the AC made it cold in the kitchen, my palms were wet with sweat.

"Guess I better go." I edged out of the room.

Mom looked up. "Do you really need to smell like a room full of flowers for pizza with the girls?"

"Mom," I said.

Her perfect lipstick lips smiled. "Come on, Caroline, no need to be shy, you can tell me if there are going to be boys there. When I was your age, I had a different boyfriend every week."

I shrugged. "Mom, please."

"Caroline likes a boy," Dicky said, and I wanted to smack him. A pink silk scarf that belonged to Jess was draped around his neck. His small hand rhythmically stroked it.

"Cool scarf." I smirked.

He frowned at me, his gaze so intense his eyes almost crossed.

Mom laughed. "I think it suits him." It had been a long time since I'd heard her laugh. For one second I wished I wasn't going out; that I could sit in the kitchen with them, that Dad would come home with a kiss for Mom, that everything would be like it used to be. I stared down at the black mirrors of my shoes, and Tony's poem came to mind: "There is darkness in the rain. Darkness touching every living thing." And I thought, there is darkness in this room with all the lights on. As I turned to go, Dicky was kissing the pink scarf.

Tony smiled as if nothing in the world was wrong and kissed me when I got in the car. His mouth tasted like Juicy Fruit gum. He was wearing black pants that weren't jeans, and a neatly pressed cream-colored shirt. There was a wet shine to his dark hair. He'd dressed up for me.

We drove to a restaurant called Emilio's. I'd never been there before, but Jess had told me it was a really romantic place. As I walked in I saw that in spite of her tendency to exaggerate, what she'd said was true. Candles flickered on round tables covered with white cloths. Green wine bottles and bunches of fake grapes, their lustrous purple globes glowing in the soft light, decorated the walls. The waiter seated us at a table next to a window. It was like I was in a foreign land, distant from all my worries.

"I thought you'd like this place," Tony said as we opened our menus. He plucked a rose from the vase on the table, held it to my cheek and said, "For you." I ordered lasagna. He ordered chicken parmesan and a bottle of Chianti, "For me and my fiancée." The waiter didn't even blink.

"Fiancée?" I said.

He shrugged. "When I say that, they never ask for ID. You like red, don't you?"

I told him I did. After the waiter filled our glasses, I took a sip, trying to relax, but I could barely swallow it. My hand was closed in a tight fist. Tony uncurled my fingers one by one.

"Come on," he said. "Is it so hard to smile?"

I tried, but it was a fake smile.

He went on, "I got the car all tuned up. We'll leave for Redondo on Friday. You can tell your parents you're going to a sleepover." He paused. "Before you know it we'll be sitting here again, all three of us, sharing a bottle of wine together."

"Right." I tried to picture Jess in her red bathing suit, smiling, all of us okay, everything the way it was supposed to be.

"You still like me, don't you, Caroline?" He paused. "I think I can tell when I like a girl and she likes me, right?" He tilted his face, his smile uncertain.

I looked up. "I do."

"That's better," he said. "I got a little something for you." He reached into his pocket. I expected a ring like he'd given Edie, but he took out a small, flat box. "Go on and open it."

Inside was a blue pendant on a thin gold chain. When I looked more closely, I saw it was actually a tiny blue flower sealed in glass. "It's beautiful," I said as he lifted the necklace from the box.

"It's a forget-me-not." A chill went through me. I could never forget him. "It belonged to my mother," he said. "My real mother." I raised my eyebrows. "She died after I was born. She gave me up, but she gave me this. I guess I should be grateful." He frowned.

"It probably meant a lot to her," I said.

"I've waited years to find the right person to give it to." His fingers tickled as he fastened it around my neck.

"It's very precious to me." I smiled.

"Glad you like it." He stared at me with a hurt look on his face. It must have been so hard to be abandoned by his real mother.

When the waiter brought our food, Tony ate like a starved man. He refilled his glass from the bottle on the table. He went to refill mine, saw it was almost full, and shook his head. He held it to my lips and said, "Drink."

I took a small sip. The way the ricotta in my lasagna spilled out onto the tomato sauce looked like vomit, but I forced myself to eat some. I tried to push my thoughts of Geraldine out of my mind, but I couldn't. Each moment was like a petal peeled away from a cold flower. I was afraid of what I might learn, but at the same time I had to know.

I was amazed that Tony was able to eat calmly, as if the news about Geraldine hadn't shaken him in any way. The police must have asked him a lot of hard questions, especially if they thought the anonymous tip had come from someone he knew. I sipped more wine. He finished off his. As he wiped the last of the tomato sauce from his plate with his bread, I raised my eyes to him. "I feel so bad about Geraldine."

He leaned back. "I do, too. It's a tragedy." He refilled his glass.

I went on, "It was terrible the way they talked about you on the news, like you'd done something wrong. How can you stand it?"

He looked as if this was the craziest thing he'd ever heard. "Caroline—I mean, Caro." There was a wild shine to his eyes. He wrapped his warm hand around mine. His cheeks had a rosy glow. "Those clowns blame me for everything. I'm used to it."

"You're not worried?"

"When we get back from California with Jess, they'll be calling me a hero." He was talking too loud. The whole restaurant could probably hear him. "I can't wait until we're out of this place and on the road." His voice filled with excitement.

"I can't wait either." I forced myself to finish off the last of my wine, though I hated its sour taste.

Tony went to pour me more, but the bottle was empty. He smiled. "It's time to go dancing."

CHAPTER 24

As we walked toward the car, I glanced back at the restaurant's blinking red neon sign, wishing for the courage to ask about the shoe. I took a deep breath.

"Tony," I said.

"What, my love?" He staggered a little as he opened the car door. He'd had more to drink than I realized.

"Nothing," I said. He turned the key in the ignition and we glided out of the parking spot as if the car had wings. I leaned my head against the back of the seat, my worries trapped inside me. He whistled as he drove across an overpass, the city lights below gleaming like rhinestones on black velvet. He fiddled with the radio. Donovan sang, "Candy Man." Tony went to change it, but I told him I liked it.

He grinned. "You like it better than my songs?"

I shook my head.

"Good," he said, "'cause I am the candy man."

I smiled listening to the sweet, sad melody.

"We're going to the Hi-Ho Club." He took a turn so fast I almost fell off the seat. I couldn't believe that soon we'd be dancing. Excitement whirled inside me until I remembered I was only getting to go because Jess was missing. I wondered if my happiness would always have an undertone of sadness, just like the song.

As we drove deeper into the darkness, we flew past shadowy houses, a gas station or two, and then nothing but telephone poles. There were fewer and fewer cars on the road. I wondered where the Hi-Ho Club could possibly be. I'd thought it was on Speedway, but we were heading into the desert.

He glanced toward the glove compartment. "Open that up," he said. "I put the other white shoe in there. You can change into them before we get to the club."

I froze. "I forgot to bring the other one."

"You forgot again?"

I nodded.

He pushed his shoulders back. "That's okay. We'll stop by your house and you can sneak in and get it."

"Tony." I struggled to clear my throat. "I don't want to wear those shoes. The ones I have on are fine."

He turned to me. "No, they're not fine. I want you to wear those shoes."

I felt cold all over, and slid toward the door.

He said more quietly, "They'll look pretty on you." He went on, "It'll be okay. We'll stop and get it. You'll have no problem sneaking in. We both know your dad and mom will be too soused to notice."

Darkness stretched on either side of the lonely highway as far as I could see. I had to tell him. A nervous smile crossed my face. "I don't want to stop and get it."

He swerved to the side of the road and slammed on the brakes. Then he opened the glove compartment and pulled out the shoe. I flinched as he held it up.

"Caroline, what is your problem with this?"

"I'm sorry." Tears filled my eyes. I didn't want him to be mad at me. That was the last thing I wanted. "It's just that . . . " I stammered, "I think that's Geraldine's shoe."

He dropped it in his lap. "Caroline, why do you think this is Geraldine's shoe?"

I looked away. "I don't know."

He leaned toward me. "I think you do know." He fixed his eyes on me, blue even in the darkness. "Tell me, why is this her shoe? Come on, Caroline, lots of girls own white shoes."

I tugged on my snowflake earring. "I know that, but those white shoes came from Sears, and Geraldine's did, too, and we never shop there. Mom says only people who can't afford anything better shop at Sears." I paused. "And they have an ankle strap, and Geraldine's had an ankle strap. And . . . ." I took a deep breath. Hot tears slid from my eyes. "Her shoes are missing."

He sighed. "You have a point there."

I wiped my eyes with the back of my hand. "I meant to tell you earlier, but I didn't know how. And when you told me about your mom, you were so sad I didn't want to upset you. But I was hoping you'd be able to explain it, because I'm worried sick that Jess has done something terrible and that's why she ran away, and you're the only person I know who I can ask about this."

The silence of the desert rose up around us. Stars twinkled in the cold quiet of the night sky, so many of them; it was as if someone had shaken sugar on the darkness. He turned my face gently toward his. "I can explain, but there are some things you may not want to know."

The blue irises of his eyes were like that flower encased in glass. "I want to know," I said. "Knowing is better than not knowing."

He looked at me sadly. "Once you know something you can't unknow it."

"I need to know."

The keys jingled as he fiddled with them. I thought he might drive away without saying anything, but he turned so he was facing me. "I went out with Geraldine a couple of times. She wasn't my type, but she'd gotten it in her head that she was in love with me."

I caught my breath. So he did know her.

He rubbed his forehead. "She came to one of my parties. We all were there, Debbie, Moose, and your sister. I'd just started seeing Jess." A quick smile crossed his face. "I knew your sister was the one. We had something special. Geraldine wasn't happy about that. She followed me everywhere that night. She drove me crazy, watching me and Jess with this hurt look like she was right and we were wrong. She acted like she knew everything when she knew nothing. You know that kind of person?" He put his hand on my knee and his eyes searched mine. I worried he thought I was that type of person.

"When she saw me and Jess kissing, she began drinking White Russians." He frowned. "She got drunk, drunker than I am now." His gaze slid over me. "The last time I saw her was in the living room. She said I'd ruined her life. I tried to let her down easy. I told her I had loved her but it was over. I held her, but she wouldn't stop crying." His eyes sort of twitched and he looked away. "Jess came in and saw us together. She started screaming at Geraldine. Your sister was so jealous. She said some mean things, the way she always does." I nodded.

He went on, "Geraldine ran outside. Jess ran after her." He put his head in his hands and exhaled hard. "I found Geraldine at the bottom of the pool, Jess sitting on the edge, white as a ghost. She told me Geraldine was so drunk she fell in. I dove in and tried to save her, but Caroline . . . ." He paused. "She wasn't like me. She didn't come back to life. I held her in my arms. She was like a little rag doll." He looked down at his hands as if he were still holding her. I wanted to say something, but it felt like my throat was closing.

"Jess just sat there not saying a word, Caroline. I think it was an accident, but the way things looked, we had to get rid of the evidence. So, me, Debbie, Moose, and Jess dug a grave in the desert and buried Geraldine."

My mouth fell open. "You buried her?"

He sighed. "We had to."

"But why didn't you call the police?"

"We couldn't do that." He stared out at the desert. "They would have gotten the wrong idea."

My skin grew cold, my mouth dry. I thought I might throw up. "You did it for my sister, didn't you?"

He reached over and took my hand in his. He held it tight for a second and then said, "When we got back I found the shoes by the pool. Geraldine must have taken them off before she fell in. Jess wanted them. Not sure why, but you know how she gets when she wants something." I nodded.

"Afterward, she wouldn't talk about what happened, wouldn't even let me bring it up. It was this thing . . . ." He paused, looking up at the gray cloth ceiling. "That held us together, but I knew if I ever let her go, she would fall apart. She began having bad dreams. She believed Geraldine's ghost was haunting her." He wiped his face with his sleeve. "Sounds crazy, I know. But she *was* haunted. She couldn't get past it. And she had this weird obsession with the shoes. It was like she wore them as a reminder of what had happened. I told her it was only a matter of time before the police found out she had them, but she wouldn't listen."

I shivered. "I thought you said it was an accident."

"It was, but she felt responsible. So do I. Something like that never leaves you." He looked down. "The night she disappeared, I'd finally convinced her to bring the shoes so I could get rid of them. It would be a new start for us. But when she realized she'd forgotten one, she became hysterical. She took it as a sign that there was no escape from her suffering. She told me she was going to run away and I'd never see her again. I tried to talk her out of it but nothing worked. Caroline . . . ." He took a deep breath. "I couldn't reach her." He paused. "So I gave up. I let her go. I'm not proud of that." I felt the warm, rough touch of his hands as he pressed mine between them. "I'm worried about what she might do to herself in Redondo. I was hoping if I got rid of the shoes, and you told her they were gone for good, then she'd be all right." He let my hand go. "But I understand if you don't want to see me anymore."

I couldn't move. If only I'd noticed more about what was going on with my sister. I rubbed the glass pendant between my fingers. Life had taken everything from Tony. First his mother, and then Jess. I couldn't turn away from him, not now. I felt his sadness as if it were my own.

He went on, "One of my friends probably told the police about the grave. Everyone betrays me." He turned to me. "But they're all in this as deep as I am."

"What do you mean?"

He stared at the black sky. "Once you touch the spirits, they never let go."

"You really believe that?" I asked, but he grew quiet, his river of words gone somewhere inside him. For what felt like the longest time, he didn't say anything else. Then he opened the car door and got out.

"Where are you going?" I asked, but he didn't answer.

I hugged my knees. It was cold in the car, the only sound the faint hiss of the desert wind. In the light from the headlights I could see the ragged branches of dry scrub, cacti rising like dark hands from the silver sand, Tony walking into the darkness.

I thought of what he'd told me. No one had ever told me something like this before. No one told me anything. I pressed my mouth on my knee. I had the awful feeling he might step off the edge of the earth and leave me here alone. When I almost couldn't see him anymore, I pushed the door open and walked toward him, my shoes slipping on the gravelly sand. I quickened my step as the long dry grass where the snakes hid brushed my legs.

He was kneeling down when I approached. "Get away," he said, turning round, his face and hands streaked with dirt.

"I'm not going anywhere," I said. As I reached out to him I looked down to see the white heel of the shoe poking out of a hole in the ground. I shivered as he pushed some dirt over it. Then he took my hand and stood up.

He smiled at me sadly. "You still want to get your sister home, right?" I told him yes and we looked up at the sky, like a highway of glittering diamonds. He pulled me close and pressed his lips into my hair, his hands hot as fire where they touched me. I looked down at the white daisies on my nails.

He said, "You have stars on your hands."

"They're not stars. They're flowers." I stared off into the distance, filled with a feeling of softness I could not explain except to say it was love. I turned to him. "They once showed us a film in school of a desert bloom. It was speeded up so you could see clouds of pink and white flowers spreading across the sand."

He laced my fingers in his. "You have a nice way of saying things."

I looked up at him and smiled.

"I guess we're not going dancing tonight." He pushed the toe of his boot in the sand.

I shook my head. "I have to get home."

"That's okay." His lips brushed my ear as he whispered, "Just bring the other shoe when we leave for California. It's more important than ever that we get rid of it. Jess needs us to do that for her. And then it will be as if none of this happened." He leaned against me and as I held him up so he wouldn't fall, I wondered how it was we'd ended up in this loneliest of places.

Shortly after I got home it started to rain. As I stood by the sliding glass doors listening to it coming down, I thought of Tony's poem, and for the first time heard the darkness in the rain. It was like a thousand voices whispering the story of all the sad things that were happening in the world, of all the broken people, of all the lives that ended too soon.

I took off my shoes and stepped outside to feel the rain. Droplets pelted the dark water in the pool. As I stood at the edge, I thought of Geraldine. Did she mean to go in the pool? Was it an accident or something worse? I couldn't stop shivering. All I knew was Jess had done nothing to save her. And now she might take her own life without giving it a second thought. I didn't want to lose my sister. We had to make it to California in time.

CHAPTER 25

Though it was only a few days away, I was sorry we had to wait until Friday to leave. The thought of Jess alone in Redondo and the terrible guilt she must be feeling frightened me. I wished I'd had the courage to go when Tony first asked. But she just had to hang on a little longer.

I tried to ease my worries by doing what Tony did and foreseeing the outcome I wanted. I saw us sitting on the deck of a beach house with Jess, sipping tropical drinks and watching the red sun sink into the sea. She'd have a new boyfriend. I would be with Tony. We'd leave everything in Tucson behind, whatever Jess had done in the past erased. I'd reassure Mom and Dad that we'd come home soon, but we'd take our time. Our lives would begin again. We would pluck oranges from the trees and live in the now. The past would be a pile of blank pages scattering in the wind.

On Wednesday I joined my former friends for lunch, not even caring if they wanted me to sit with them. After all, it could be the last time I saw them. I put my tray down on the table next to May's.

I struggled with my carton of chocolate milk. "Why do things say 'open here' when that never works?" I said as I tore it open and shoved in a straw.

I glanced up. No one was smiling.

"Stop looking at me like that. It's okay, guys," I said.

Sheila glared at me. "It isn't always about you."

I almost spit out my milk. "What's wrong?"

"It's Steve," Billy said.

A blush of shame crept into my cheeks. Sheila was right. I'd been so preoccupied with my own life it had never occurred to me that someone else could have problems.

May leaned toward me. "He's coming home." She glanced at Billy. They were officially a couple now. Everyone said they might be homecoming king and queen. I didn't care. I was over that.

"That's good," I replied cautiously.

Billy sighed. "No it isn't. He lost an arm."

"He'll never play football again," May said.

Though I felt bad, I couldn't shake the sense that she was rubbing in how wrong I was.

I tried to get Billy to look at me, but he wouldn't. "That's terrible. I'm sorry." I wanted to leave the table, rush into the hall, out of the school, out of the world, out of the universe.

Finally Billy said, "At least he's alive. And he got a Purple Heart."

"Then he's a hero," I said. "You must be so proud."

I couldn't believe I was repeating the same phony thing everyone said whenever someone joined up, but Billy smiled solemnly at me and said, "Thank you." He paused. "It's just an arm. A person can live without an arm." The table became painfully quiet.

After school, while walking out in a crowd of kids, I caught a glimpse of Tony's car parked in front. He's come for me, I thought with a surge of excitement, and was about to run to him when a police car pulled up behind him. I felt a pain in my stomach.

Billy waved to me. He was standing in front of his mom's car. I went over to him. "Come on, we'll give you a ride," he said, wiping some sweat from above his mouth. I looked back to see a policeman shoving Tony up against the car.

"Caroline, nice to see you again," Billy's mom said. "I'm sure Billy told you the good news. Our Steven's coming home." She turned to me with a stiff smile. Moms who suffered always had to be brave and carry on. I'd learned that this summer.

"I'm so glad." I craned my neck to get a better look at Tony. The police cruiser rolled slowly down the street. He was getting back into his car. He turned, his simmering eyes resting on me a second before he drove away.

"Caroline, would you mind if I drop you two off at The Flying Saucer for a snack while I do an errand?" Billy's mom said.

"That's fine," I said. Much as I hated The Flying Saucer, it would help pass the time while I waited for it to be Friday.

Billy hardly said a word as we ate our french fries. It was strange being with him, knowing what I knew and not being able to tell him. I pushed my blonde hair behind my ears. I was a new person, someone he could never understand. From this time forward it would be as if we lived in two different worlds. As I dipped a fry in ketchup, I already felt far away.

I fingered the necklace Tony had given me. I hadn't taken it off since that night. "Where's May?" I asked.

"Art club, chorus, who knows? She's always got something going on." He lowered his eyes. "I'm sorry you and I haven't gotten to talk much lately."

I said, "Me too," but I didn't mean it. Billy was part of my past. May was, too. Everyone was except for Tony. He was my now.

He took a deep breath. "I'm glad Steve is coming home. You must have been relieved when you found out it wasn't Jess."

"I was, but someone still died." I stared at the bug-eyed green aliens painted on the walls. There were so many ugly things in the world, but before all this happened none of them had been real to me. Now it was like the terrible things Tony had said in the desert were inside me, and I would never be able to see anything the same way again. I remembered coming up on him, his hands buried in the sand, the agonized look on his face. It was like he was still with me as I was sitting here, his eyes always watching, knowing. Something about him was so strange, it was almost like *he* came from outer space or another world, and now that I knew him, that other world was part of me too.

"I guess we might never find out what happened to Geraldine." Billy's eyes met mine. I felt sick. He pushed his fries around on his plate. "It must be hard for you, still not knowing where Jess is."

I wanted to tell him that I knew what had happened to Geraldine, and I knew where Jess was, but I couldn't. I had to keep the awful secret that Tony and Jess shared or I might never find her.

"It is." I looked away so he wouldn't see the tears blurring my eyes.

"You still looking for real magic?" When I didn't answer he said, "I've perfected the disappearing coin trick." I turned around to see him holding up a quarter. "Want me to show you?"

I frowned. "I'm not that interested in magic anymore."

He put the coin back in his pocket quickly as if he were embarrassed. "You seem different."

I stared at my nails. "I guess I am."

He hesitated. "Did you see the police shaking down your boyfriend?"

I twisted the necklace around my finger. "He's not my boyfriend."

"He's such a loser." Billy looked at me.

"He didn't do anything wrong," I said. Billy was staring at me like *I'd* done something wrong. He was so infuriating. "You don't understand him."

Billy leaned forward. "What's there to understand?"

I shoved my plate away. There was no point in talking to him, but if I didn't defend Tony no one would. Everyone was betraying him. "He's all alone in the world with Jess gone. His real mother abandoned him."

Billy shook his head. "That's what he told you."

"It's true."

He folded his arms on the table. "You can think whatever you want, but he's lying."

I stood up. "I don't have to listen to this."

Billy held my wrist, the touch of his fingers dry and cool. "Caroline, that guy is a worthless piece of shit."

I tried to pull away but the tears that had been building up inside me spilled out. "You're wrong. No one understands him the way I do. There's a whole other side to him. He's helping me find my sister."

Billy eyed me uncomfortably. "You all right?" he said.

"It's nothing. I cry all the time now."

Billy touched my shoulder. "I know what you're going through."

I shrugged. "Steve's alive and he's coming home. You have no idea what I'm going through."

He pressed his thumbs together. "Until last week, I didn't know if Steve was dead or alive. I *do* know how you feel." I gave him a hard look. "Come on. Let's pay the bill," he said with a nervous laugh. I refused to look at him as we went over to the cashier.

As I was reaching for my money, I caught my breath. Geraldine's mother was sitting at the register, as if this were any other day and not less than a week since her daughter's body had been found. I handed Billy my money and stood behind him, hoping she wouldn't remember who I was, but as she counted out his change, she stared straight at me. Her saggy face looked so soft it seemed like if you touched it your hand might sink in forever.

Was that what grief was like—forever? I averted my eyes, but she kept staring. Her hand went to the green silk scarf knotted at her throat. I worried that without my saying a word, she knew what Tony had told me.

"I'm so sorry for your loss," I murmured.

"Thank you, darling." Her eyes were still on me, the look in them not recognition, but something else that made me uneasy. "Come here," she said.

Billy raised his eyebrows as I edged over to the counter. When I was standing across from her she reached out and touched the pendant. "Geraldine had a necklace just like this." The touch of her fingers on my neck was like ice. I could see the worm-like veins on the back of her hand. She was staring at it intensely, almost as if she thought it was Geraldine's, but it wasn't possible.

"It was a gift." My voice shook.

She let it go. "You're a pretty girl like my Geraldine." She went on, "Everywhere I look, I see things that remind me of her."

"I'm really sorry," I mumbled, almost tripping as I stepped back, my thoughts going a thousand miles a minute. This didn't make sense. Tony couldn't have gotten the necklace from Geraldine. He'd gotten it from his mother.

One of the waitresses came over. "Is everything all right here?"

Geraldine's mom said, "As all right as it can ever be." I hesitated, her eyes pulling me into their black whirlpools of sorrow.

"Galvin," Billy called out in an exasperated voice. He was standing by the door. I ran towards him as if for dear life.

I got into Billy's mom's car like someone in a trance. Though it was light and delicate, the pendant rested heavily on my neck. Outside the car window, everything looked the same—the same sun, same green yards, same whirling sprinklers—but nothing was the same. From now on every shadow could twist into a snake; every sparkle could become a stolen jewel; every beautiful white shoe could belong to someone who'd died.

When we got to Billy's, his mom went in their house, but he stayed outside with me.

"Are you okay?" he asked. I couldn't speak. He had no idea. Something was unbearably wrong. If this was Geraldine's necklace then Tony was lying, and I had no idea what else he'd lied about. But to doubt what I felt for him was to doubt the most important thing I'd ever known. It was as if someone had told me the sky was green, not blue.

Billy moved closer to me. "I hope that lady in the restaurant didn't creep you out too much."

"She did, a little." I forced a smile.

"I've been thinking," he said. I looked up at him. "About that time Tony almost drove me off the road."

"I'm sure he didn't mean to do it. It was dark. He must not have seen you." I bit my lip so hard it hurt. "I've got to go," I said.

"Not yet." He touched my arm. "I don't know what he told you, but the more I think about it, the more I'm sure it was Jess with him in the car that night."

I flipped my hair over my shoulder. "She forgot something. He was driving her to his house to get it."

"But then why was she screaming?"

"She was mad at him because of Edie, that's all." I glanced away, wishing I could tell Billy what she was really upset about, but I couldn't.

"That's what he told you. You don't know that it's true."

I turned back to him, trying to ignore the panic roaring through me. "Not everything is a lie," I said, though at that moment even the ground beneath my feet felt like one. I wished he'd go already but he remained stubbornly beside me.

"You don't have to rely on Tony to help you find Jess. I can help you." There was something sweet about his offer, but he had no idea how wrong he was. Tony and I were the only ones who could find my sister.

"I don't need your help." I stared at him. His tan blurred his freckles together, and he'd grown even taller and more handsome since the start of the summer. I wished I could listen to him and like him the way I used to, but I couldn't. "Why don't you go talk to May?"

"Caroline," he said, "this is about you, not her. I'm worried about you."

"Why?"

He squinted up at the sky. "Moose told me something."

"Moose? Since when are you talking to Moose?"

"Since I went undercover. He said you're going to California with Tony on Friday, and he told me to warn you not to go."

I glared at him. "He's lying."

"Is he?"

"Jesus Christ, Moose is a criminal. Didn't you know that? For all I know, he's the one who killed Geraldine."

Billy dug his hands into his pockets. "Moose isn't the criminal. Tony is."

Though it was warm out, I was cold all over. I almost couldn't feel my body. It was as if I wasn't even there, or anywhere. I reached up and touched the necklace. "There are things I know that I can't tell you about, but by next week you'll understand. Everyone will."

His eyes searched mine. "You're going, aren't you?"

"Please, Billy." I was angry with myself for giving away too much. "Don't tell anyone or you'll ruin everything."

He stood there a moment and then headed toward his house.

In my room I put the necklace back in the box, and resolved never to wear it again. I tried to convince myself that Tony had merely exaggerated its value. It was probably neither unusual nor precious. I remembered him saying, "Lots of girls have white shoes." Maybe lots of girls had blue flower necklaces, too. I couldn't really make myself believe that, but I had no choice. Jess was in Redondo, and we had to get there as soon as possible. No matter what turned out to be true, I couldn't back out now. I had to save her.

I sank down on my bed and held my hand over my heart. It was pushing against my ribs, like it was being squeezed. I worried I might be having a heart attack. Young people in perfect health sometimes simply dropped dead. Perhaps my fate was to die tragically, my love for Tony forever unfulfilled. I thought of the rain falling the night before, the two of us alone in the desert, the warmth of his cheek against mine. I reached for the box and touched the smooth glass pendant one last time. It was cool, as if there was a little bit of rain trapped in it.

If this was Geraldine's necklace, why on earth would Tony have given it to me? Maybe she'd left it in his house, and he didn't know it belonged to her. But then why had he lied to me about it being from his mother? I thought of the pain I'd seen in his eyes, the pain he didn't want me to see. Like all of us, he was just a little broken. I wrapped my arms around myself, feeling like I was broken. Only one thing was certain: I couldn't let my doubts unravel everything when we were so close to finding Jess.

Reluctantly, I began to pack my canvas bag. It felt strange doing this without Mom looking over my shoulder and reminding me of embarrassing things like bringing enough underwear. I tried again to picture what I wanted to happen, us sitting around a bamboo table, the sea churning far below, Jess twirling the tiny umbrella from her drink, and Tony with his hand on the back of my chair, touching me ever so lightly. I was hiding my bag under the bed when the phone rang.

I picked it up. It was him.

As soon as he said, "Hello," it was as if a wind had blown all my worries away.

"Did you see what happened at the school?"

I told him I had and he said, "You know what I think?"

"What?"

"I think someday those guys are gonna kill me."

His words sent an ache through me. "Don't say that."

He paused. "You have fun with lover-boy today?"

"Billy's mom just gave me a ride home."

"You still like him?"

"Who?"

"Billy."

"You know I don't." I wound a pink thread from my bedspread around my finger.

"So are we still on for Friday?"

I told him yes. What else could I say? He would pick me up at "our spot" at the end of the street on Friday night at seven. I'd tell my mom that I was going to sleep over at Sheila's house. Tony and I would leave Arizona behind in a wake of dust.

CHAPTER 26

Finally it was Friday. After school, I sat in the kitchen eating an apple. Mom sat down next to me. She fidgeted with a napkin and smiled oddly as if she knew something was up. I hoped she wasn't going to say I couldn't go to the sleepover. I'd made sure to tell her ahead of time so there was no chance my plans with Tony would fall apart.

As I took a bite she said, "I saw the photo of Jess you left on her bureau."

A wave of panic went through me. Had she figured out I was going to California? "Mom," I said, "you're not supposed to go through my private stuff."

She clasped her hands in front of her on the table. "Sorry, honey. I was just tidying up." I put down my apple. "You don't have to be embarrassed. I understand how it might make you feel better to look at pictures of Jess. It makes me feel better, too."

She smiled sadly in her silky gray dress. A wide silver belt cinched her waist. Though no one was around except for Dicky and me, she was wearing perfume. I felt sorry for her because she was the sort of person who got dressed up every day for something special that never happened. I wasn't going to be that sort of person. I was done waiting. Whatever happened, at least I would know that I'd tried.

As she rearranged some metal canisters that were already neatly arranged, I wished I could tell her about California, about

Tony, and ask her about love, and whether I was doing the right thing, and all those other things that always froze on my lips whenever she turned to me, but all I said was, "You look pretty."

She smiled. "Your dad and I are going to the Beckhams' for dinner tonight."

I stared at her. "But you said I could go to the sleepover."

"Don't worry. We're bringing Dicky so you don't have to babysit, unless you want to."

"Not really." I crunched into my apple. Thank God I'd said the sleepover was at Sheila's house and not May's.

"I didn't think you would." She fixed her eyes on me. "It's okay for you to have some fun sometimes. You know that, don't you?"

"I know, Mom," I said.

She ran her finger along a shiny metal canister. I was glad she and Dad were going out. It had been a while since they'd done anything together. When I brought Jess home, they might even fall back in love. I guess I'd known for some time that they weren't in love anymore. It was nothing anyone said, just something I knew, the way you know a storm is coming, or snow.

They left before I did and that was perfect, because I didn't have to worry about Mom asking too many questions. I put on jeans and a shirt the color of California sunshine. I wanted to smash the pendant, but I left it in its little box, the blue glass flower sleeping on the cotton batting. If Tony really loved me, he would explain his lie. Until then, I had to push my doubts aside and concentrate on finding my sister.

As I put on my makeup, I thought back to the night when Jess had climbed out the window, and remembered her saying, "Would you," in that breathy impatient voice of hers. She would want me to find her. She would not want me to give up.

I brushed on some peach blush, and once again felt Tony's light touch on my cheek, the memory more unsettling than reassuring. I tried to steady my nerves as I dragged my canvas bag from under my bed and packed a few more things. When I was almost done, I went over to the closet to get the shoe. While she was tidying, Mom had lined all of our shoes up against the back wall. The thought of her going through my things was a little annoying. I looked around, but I couldn't find it. It had to be there. I tossed things around frantically, but I didn't see it.

I pulled a chair over and looked on the top shelf above the rod with the hangers. There were old report cards, board games like Sorry! and Parcheesi, but no shoe. I glanced at my watch. It was almost time to go. I was practically hyperventilating as I wondered how I was going to explain this to Tony. Maybe I'd tell him my mom had thrown it away. He wouldn't want to hear that, but if I waited much longer I might be late. As I was rushing around, I almost tripped over a laundry basket Mom had left in the middle of the room. She'd filled it with my clothes and some of Jess's. It was so odd, but also typical of Mom to decide to do Jess's laundry now. I pictured her going through Jess's things, staring at each item a little too long. As I glanced over at her bed one last time, I felt a catch in my throat. Mr. Rabbit was gone. Mom must have put him back in Dicky's room.

When I opened the front door Linda was dropping May and Sheila off at Billy's. I was relieved that they went inside without noticing me. I locked the house up as I'd promised Mom I would, and shoved my ruby-slipper keychain into my purse. As I stood waiting on the sidewalk, my bag was heavy, even without the shoe.

When Tony pulled up, he got out of the car and held the door for me. I put my bag on the floor. He slid in next to me, his sweaty arm pressed against mine. He was wearing a white sleeveless undershirt. The red bandana tied around his head made him look like a pirate. He smiled. We sat for a moment, thinking of the road ahead. Then he drew me close and kissed me, his breath tainted with the sweet, sick smell of whiskey. I pulled away.

"What's wrong?" he said.

I touched my throat, thinking of the necklace, wishing he'd explain. "Nothing."

He jutted out his lower lip. "I'm sorry for having a drink. It's just the thought of seeing your sister again scares me."

I knotted my fingers together. "It scares me, too."

His arm brushed up against me as he reached into the glove compartment. "I've got something that will make you happy."

"What?" I didn't want another gift.

He handed me a postcard. "This came yesterday. I thought you'd want to see it."

I took it from him. It had a picture of Schwab's Pharmacy on the front like the one Jess had left on the bureau, only there was a big difference. She'd written something on this one. He switched on the dome light. I could barely make out her tiny writing as I read:

Dear Tony,

Having a great time. Brian took me to Hollywood. We saw the stars in the sidewalk at Grauman's Chinese Theatre but the very best was Schwab's Pharmacy. Wish you were here.

Love,

Jess

An unexpected feeling of hope, out of place in the sweat-and-whiskey-scented car, rose up inside me. Maybe Jess really had left the card on the bureau as a sign, and sending a message using the same type of card was another sign. To anyone else it would appear to be just a postcard, but I could see what she really meant.

"She's saying she wants us to come get her." My voice was tinged with excitement. She was going to wait for us. She would be there.

Tony nodded. "That's what I thought, too. It's the first I've heard from her since that night."

We sat in the dim light, his arm around me. Though neither of us would say it for fear of jinxing things, we both felt the presence of fate. Everything was happening the way it was supposed to.

I slipped the postcard into my pocket and leaned my face against the window as he drove down my street to the place where the new housing development ended, beyond it only dry scrub and sand. It was like God had started drawing a picture with kids, bikes, and houses, and then stopped. I used to pretend sometimes that this was the end of the world, but before I knew it we were speeding past it, on a dark highway running straight through the desert, the only sound the roar of the engine. When we'd driven a little while, he pulled over to the side of the road.

"Do you a need to check a map?" I asked.

He frowned. "I know how to get there. Reach in your bag and get the shoe. We have to get rid of it before we go any farther."

I took a deep breath. "It's not in there."

"What do you mean?"

"My mom cleaned my room and I couldn't find it. I think she threw it away." I tried to smile.

His eyes widened. "She threw it away?"

"I'm not sure, but I couldn't find it anywhere. All that matters is it's gone, right?"

"That's not all that matters. You know that there is more to this than either of us understands. We have to be sure we've gotten rid of that shoe before we go to California." He paused. "Otherwise things might not turn out as planned." The intensity of his gaze made me squirm.

"What am I supposed to do?" I said.

"I'll take you home and you can look one more time. I have a feeling you're going to find it." He ran his finger down my neck and rested it on my shirt button. "Okay?"

I was embarrassed because I was breathing too loud. He tapped on the steering wheel, waiting for my answer.

"All right," I said. "At least my parents are out."

While I went inside, he stayed in the car with it running in case we had to make a fast getaway. We arranged that if by some chance my parents showed up, he would drive around the corner and I'd meet him there. As I turned the key in the door I stole a look at him.

"Go on." He smiled.

The house was silent except for the low hum of the air conditioner. The single light burning in the hall illumined the mail neatly piled on the table by the mirror—bills, an advertisement for a Ford Mustang. I walked through the darkened living room, went upstairs, and turned on my pink lamp.

I looked in the closet again, went through the stuff I'd already tossed around, and then I saw it. Mom had placed the shoe neatly on top of the other ones in the back. I'd missed it earlier, though it was right in front of me. I breathed a sigh of relief as I grabbed it, and opened the window. "Found it," I called out, and held it up so he could see.

As I stepped away I knocked over the laundry basket, scattering clothes everywhere. One of Jess's favorite shirts was lying at my feet. Looking at it gave me a sick feeling. As I stooped to pick it up, I saw something red underneath it. I pulled out the top to her red bathing suit, the same one she was wearing in the photo Tony had given me. I felt like someone had punched me in the stomach.

I picked up the photo from the bureau, praying that my eyes had played tricks on me and she would turn out to be wearing a different one, but she was wearing the same red bathing suit. I could even see the little rose where it fastened in front. I wondered what else I'd missed. The cloud-dusted sky could be a sky anywhere. The people sitting around her were all blurred strangers, Jess the center of attention as always, but behind her in the distance I could just make out a curved shape resting on a tracery of spidery lines. I looked closer. It had to be the roller coaster at Paragon Park. We often went there after a day at the beach back east. I felt like I was on that roller coaster now, barreling down an incline. I clutched her bathing suit to my chest.

My hands trembled as I took the postcard out of my pocket, held it under the lamp and read it again. In the bright light it didn't even look like her handwriting. I turned it over and touched the place where the stamp should have been. There was no postmark. As I dropped it on the floor, I wanted to cry, I felt like such a fool. Tony must have written it. Or maybe he'd gotten Edie to. The only thing I was sure of was that Jess hadn't sent the postcard, and she wasn't in California.

I sank down on the pink rug, and tried to breathe more slowly so I could think. There was the necklace, what Edie said about Tony killing a girl, what Billy had said about seeing Jess in Tony's car. How many other things were there that I'd failed to notice?

Tony honked impatiently. If Jess wasn't in California, where were we going? I picked up the shoe. Maybe he'd have an explanation for all of this. My stomach sank—another explanation. The only one that made sense was too terrible to believe.

I went over to the window again. He'd gotten out of the car and was standing below, looking up at me, his face masked in shadows. He called out, "Are you ready?"

I stared at him grimly, not knowing what to do. "I'll be down in a minute," I said. He walked toward our front door. I ran downstairs, through the dimly lit living room, and into the front hall with its coat rack bereft of coats, its single light still burning. My heart hammered in my chest. I was still holding the shoe. I dropped it on the floor. Feet scuffed on the front step. I went over to the door, hesitated, and latched it.

From the other side I heard him say, "Caroline, you there?"

As the doorknob turned, I was breathing so hard I could barely utter the word, "Yes."

The doorknob turned again. "What are you doing? Caroline, open the door."

I pressed my face against the smooth panel of white wood separating me from him. I could almost feel his large hand as he grasped the brass doorknob, and his heavy boots on the step. Those blue eyes on the other side would never reassure me again. "My parents are coming home soon. You need to go."

"They aren't coming home soon."

I stepped back, the doorknob still turning this way and that. "You can't come in."

It stopped moving. "Did you lock this?"

"I did."

"Why?"

"I don't know."

"Jesus Christ, what is the matter?" He pressed his eye against the small peephole in the door.

I caught my breath. "I know what you did."

I heard him stepping back. There was a silence and then he said slowly, "What did I do?"

The door was reflected at an angle in the round hall mirror, like something in a funhouse. Everything in the room felt twisted and strange.

I tried to keep my voice steady. "You lied about the postcard. Jess didn't write it. You did."

"So what?" It was like he was biting off each word. "It's nothing. It's a postcard. I wanted to make you happy."

I went on, "You lied about the photo of California, too. I found the bathing suit she was wearing in the picture in my room."

He sighed loudly. "It's just a photo. Come on, let me in."

"I can't."

"Why are you doing this to me?" he said. "I thought we were a team. I didn't want you to worry about Jess. That's why I faked the photo."

"I don't believe you." I looked down. My small feet in my shiny black shoes looked like they didn't belong to me. Tears streamed down my face.

He tried the door again, shaking it. "Why not?"

"Because you lie about everything," I said through sobs. "Nothing about you is real. I bet you're not even a good swimmer. You're nothing."

"Caroline, I am not nothing," he shouted.

"Please be quiet," I said. "Someone will hear you."

There was a pause. "You think anyone's listening, that anyone cares? News flash, Twinkle Toes, everyone in happy town is drunk or asleep. No one listens here. I'm not the fake. This whole world is fake." There was not a drop of love in his voice, just a coldness that tore my heart to pieces.

I tried to hold myself together. "No, *you* are the fake. You lied about the necklace. It didn't belong to your mother. It belonged to Geraldine."

I waited for his answer but everything became quiet. There were no cars, no sirens, no televisions. Even the ringing in my ears stopped. I shuffled backward, my shoes whispering on the carpet. Outside, a branch cracked. Leaves rustled by the picture window.

Was it locked? I didn't know. I turned toward the kitchen. The sliding glass door might have been left open. We often did that. That was how Jess always snuck back in.

There was a thundering crash. The whole door shook. He kicked it again. The sound reverberated all around me, as if the walls of the house were as thin as the sides of a cardboard box holding a diorama.

"You little fool," he said. "I s'pose next you're gonna say I killed Geraldine, that I drowned her. Is that the evil thought in your little pink flower brain? Is it?"

I backed up. My heart slowed. Oh God, what had he done?

He pounded on the door. "You think you know everything, but you don't. You know nothing." He smashed the door again. "You're a stupid little girl. I loved your sister. You're nothing like her. If you don't want to come, I'll get her myself and you'll never see either of us again."

"She isn't in California." I froze.

He lowered his voice. "Just let me in. I'll take you where she is, but we've got to leave now."

I looked back at the kitchen. Moonlight fell on a sugar bowl, the clock-patterned wallpaper. I didn't want to go where Jess was. She wasn't anywhere.

"No," I said. "You have to go home."

He shouted, "Let me in now." His voice was so loud it made my head hurt. He hit the door over and over like some kind of madman. I feared he would break it down. I put my hands on my ears. He stopped. The knob moved again. He was working something between the door and the frame. The lock jiggled. I stepped back until I was standing in the kitchen. I held my breath. My hand shook as I opened the drawer beneath the sink and slid a paring knife into my pocket. I reached for the phone, but then the front door opened. I dropped the receiver, pushed aside the sliding glass door, and ran out into the backyard.

I looked around frantically. The only way out was to climb the fence. I rushed over, and tried to hoist myself up. My feet slid against the wood. The pointed slats on top hurt my hands. I couldn't do it. I wasn't strong enough. I hung there hoping if I remained still he wouldn't see me. The sliding glass door smacked against the frame. I held my breath.

"Caroline," he called out.

I was almost over the top when I felt his hands around my waist. He pulled me down and turned me to face him.

He smiled. "What are you running from? It's just me." He didn't look like himself. His bandana was twisted and his eyes had a broken-glass look as if he wasn't seeing me or anything else. He grabbed my wrist. "You're still coming with me, right?"

"I guess." I looked down.

"What did you say?" he said sharply.

"Yes," I said.

He stared at me. "Better. You be good now, and do as I say. Geraldine never listened. Jess didn't, either, but I know you will." He tightened his grasp. "Jess only brought one shoe that night. She did it on purpose. She left the other one with you. She did that on purpose, too."

"What do you mean?" I said.

"You know what I mean. I gave you the necklace like I gave Jess the shoes. You're as deep in this as if you'd pushed Geraldine under the water, and kept pushing until she didn't come up, with your own bare hands."

I felt myself grow cold. "You gave Jess the shoes?"

"Yeah." He looked away.

"Where is she?" My voice was a dry whisper.

"You know where she is." He leaned so close his lips brushed my cheek.

"I don't know," I shouted, trying to twist free. "All I know is what the police said was true. Geraldine broke up with you, so you killed her. You couldn't stand the thought of someone not loving you."

His slap came hot against my face. "If that's what you think, you're more of a fool than I thought you were." He laughed, holding my wrist so tight it hurt. "It was an accident. The little freak should have watched her step." His gaze was unflinching.

"Let me go." I tried to pull away. He slapped me again.

When I started to scream, he put his hand over my mouth. "Take it easy," he said. "No point trying to run away. I found the shoe. It's over there on that table. We got everything we need. We can leave now." I looked toward it. All I could see were the small moon-washed oranges dangling from the gnarled tree.

I felt for the knife in my pocket. "I don't want to go."

"I know that. But you're still going." He smiled as if this was the happiest thing. He lifted my chin.

I was crying.

"Don't you worry, where we're going, honey, everything will be a lot more real." He brushed my sweaty hair from my face. "There now." He kissed my forehead, and stared past me at the pool. I felt as if the slightest breath of air might blow me away, but there was no air. My mind filled with crazy thoughts—I would never go to prom, never graduate, Jess in the front seat of the car rubbing her hands in her red mittens, her blonde braids, frost on the window.

His grip was like iron as he dragged me toward the pool. We stopped at the very edge. The water was black and still. He ran his hands through my hair. His thick fingers traced the tendons in my throat.

"Leave me alone," I screamed.

"Be quiet. If you stay quiet, nothing bad will happen," he said, but I couldn't stop screaming.

He took off his bandana. As he tied it around my mouth, there was a look in his eyes as if he wasn't here but someplace else, and I wasn't here, either, but far away with him. He smiled sadly as he knotted it tight. "You're such a little thing. You can scream all you want. You can talk all you want. No one will ever hear you now."

He pulled me up against him. My fingers tightened on the handle of the knife. As his hands closed around my neck, I stared into his blue-flower eyes, and shoved the knife into his stomach. The slippery feeling of the blade going in sickened me. His warm blood ran all over my hand. He staggered backward.

"What did you do?" There was a look of surprise on his face as if he couldn't believe that I, of all people, had done this to him. "I can't die." He looked down at the dark stain spreading across his shirt and clutched his stomach. Something passed between us, soft as a breeze or a ghost.

I turned and ran. When I reached the mesquite tree in the front yard, I looked around to see if he was following me, but he wasn't. I thought of going back into the house to call the police, but what if he was in there? I was about to dash across the street to Billy's when my parents' car pulled up. Doors were flung open. Light spilled on the sidewalk. Mom came running toward me, followed by Dad carrying Dicky. I pulled off the bandana.

"Caroline," Mom called out. "Are you all right?"

"I am." Tears were running down my face, but I felt a million miles away. I dropped the knife in the grass.

She touched my cheek with the cool tip of her finger. "Billy saw Tony's car in front of our house. He called us at the Beckhams' and told us that you weren't with May and Sheila, you were going to California with Tony. Is that true?"

I turned away. "We were going there to find Jess."

"Oh, honey." Mom reached for my hand, but as she pulled me toward her, she shrieked, "Is that blood? Are you bleeding?"

Dad put my brother down and leaned in close, his face sweaty and pale. "Caroline, are you hurt?"

I shook my head. Mom kept asking me what happened but I couldn't speak. The whole world around me—the crooked branches of the mesquite tree, the pearl glow from Billy's living room, the paving stones on our walkway, the dark blades of grass—I was grateful for all of it, but at the same time none of it felt real. A faint breeze toyed with the black leaves, and I worried that nothing would ever feel real again.

Dad glanced toward the street. "That's Tony's car. Where is he?"

Mom gripped my shoulders. "Where's Tony?"

I nodded toward the backyard. "He's there. He tried to kill me." The words felt unreal as they left my lips.

"Stay here." Dad propelled himself past us.

As he rushed toward the backyard, Mom yelled, "Please, Jack, don't go back there alone."

He turned to her. "I can handle this."

All I could think of was Tony lying by the pool, dead.

Mom held me so close I could smell the dull sweetness of her perfume, feel her silky dress against my face. I couldn't stop shaking. "I don't know what I would have done if I'd lost you," she said.

Dad came back a few moments later. "No sign of him," he said. "All I found was this." He held up the white shoe. "We better call the police."

We waited while Dad searched the house for Tony, and then went inside. As I washed the blood off my hands in the kitchen, the pink water going down the drain made me gag. I looked out the window at the backyard. Lavender moonlight, like chips of nail polish, flecked the pool. I felt a twinge inside that was part sorrow and part fear. Tony wasn't lurking in the shadows. He wasn't waiting for me.

We were sitting in the living room when the police arrived. While one policeman looked around outside, I told Officer Barnes everything, even the parts I'd lied about before.

His pale eyes met mine when I said, "Tony was going to take me to California to find Jess. But he lied to me about her. I don't know where she is. And I'm pretty sure he killed Geraldine." I looked around the room, my heart racing wildly. "He tried to kill me too, so I stabbed him." I expected him to arrest me on the spot, but all he did was nod and tell me to go on. I felt weird showing him the blue necklace, the white shoe, the photo, the postcard, the red bathing suit, but he told me I was a big help. He dropped them one by one into a plastic bag, like words in a crazy, jumbled-up poem I would never understand.

When I finished, he shook his head. "You're lucky to be alive." He rested his hand on mine. "You're very brave." I looked into my parents' stunned faces.

The other policeman came in with the blood-smeared knife in its own plastic bag. They waited with us for a tow truck to take Tony's car away.

The room fell silent after they left. It was the sort of silence that we would have avoided in the past, but now we had no choice but to bear it. Finally Dad asked if I really was all right. I told him I was, though as I spoke, it was like it wasn't my voice, and I was looking at everything—Mom, Dad, Dicky, the blank television screen, the yellow curtains framing the darkness—from far away.

A few hours later the police called to tell us they'd found Tony hitchhiking out of Tucson and arrested him. His wound was minor.

EPILOGUE

Two years had passed since Tony was sentenced to life in prison for killing Geraldine Keanen. I thought about him sometimes, wondered what he was doing in jail. Did he write poems to pass the time? Did girls write to him? Did he ever think of me or Jess? My sister was still missing.

My parents hardly ever talked about her anymore. Once in a while Dad added some photos of her to the ones already on the mantel, or to the photo cube on the coffee table—on each side, there she was. Sometimes Mom would mention how Jess could have been a movie star. Sometimes I was afraid that I was already forgetting her.

Just recently Tony had lost his appeal for a new trial. That was a huge relief. I'd worried they'd let him out and everything that had been taken away from me would be taken away again. He was supposed to be interviewed on the news at noon. As I sat on the couch trying to do my homework, I kept glancing at my watch. I hated him, but there were times when I'd remember the soft touch of his hand, the sadness in his eyes, and wonder how he could have done what he did.

I learned many things at the trial, but not everything I wanted to know. My testimony about the shoes and the necklace turned out to be the key to putting Tony in jail. After I testified, other kids came forward. Debbie and Moose admitted to helping Tony bury Geraldine. They said they were there when he drowned her but they had nothing to do with it. Debbie claimed she didn't come forward sooner because she was afraid. I didn't for one minute believe that. Debbie wasn't afraid of anything.

It turned out that Moose had called the police about the body. He was sure that Tony was going to kill Edie, and he couldn't let that happen.

Neither of them said that Jess was there when Geraldine died.

No one even mentioned her until Edie took the stand. I wanted to cover my ears and make it all go away, but I had to listen. Edie testified that she'd called Jess on the day she disappeared and told her that the white shoes belonged to Geraldine. When the lawyer asked how Edie knew they were Geraldine's shoes, she told him, "Lots of kids knew about the shoes. Jess was probably the only one who didn't know."

She pushed her green ring up and down on her thin finger and added, "Jess shouldn't have made such a scene that night. She shouldn't have told Tony she was going to the police. Everyone knew you didn't say something like that to him."

What I found out next was worse. Linda testified that after Tony and Jess fought about the shoes that night, Jess said she was taking the bus to California. Tony took Linda aside and asked her to pretend to drive her to the bus stop but to drop her off at a gas station along the highway instead. He'd meet them there. He wanted one more chance to convince Jess not to leave.

Linda watched the two of them drive off into the darkness, and that was the last she saw of my sister. On the stand she cried and said how sorry she was for not saying anything sooner, but Tony had threatened that if she breathed a word about this he'd do the same thing to her he'd done to Geraldine.

Tony didn't testify. As he sat at the front of the courtroom in his suit, every now and then he'd make a remark to his lawyer or scribble something on a piece of paper. Not once did he look at me.

In the weeks that followed they searched for Jess in the miles of desert around the gas station. Some high-school kids even helped. Eventually, they gave up. It was such a vast place, and there was no sign of her.

Now, as I sat on the couch, images from the trial swirled in my mind—Debbie walking to the stand with her arms by her side, her strangely muted voice and the way nothing seemed to touch her, Edie's white hair, Linda's red car, the ghost of sunlight on the window—like pieces of a puzzle that still wouldn't come together.

It was almost noon, so I turned on the television. Tony had been in the news a lot since the trial. Some people called him a monster. Others speculated that he had brain damage from almost drowning, or that drugs had made him do what he'd done. He remained a mystery to me. I thought of the infinite darkness I'd seen in him. Jess had seen it, too. It had touched both of us. I'd unraveled enough of the mystery to save myself, but I hadn't found her.

Dicky curled up next to me and began doing his homework. I opened my English book to Keats's "Ode to a Nightingale." I loved poetry more than ever now, especially the intricate, formal kind, the words like flowers strewn on stone, the marble solidity of it. It was about something that would always be there, something that couldn't be taken from me without warning. I planned to study poetry when I went to college in the fall. As I underlined "I have been half in love with easeful Death," the interview began.

I sat up. I hadn't seen Tony since the sentencing two years ago. He looked different, almost like someone I'd never known. His hair was cut short and his eyebrows seemed too thick and dark, but his blue eyes were still the same. When asked if he had anything to say for himself, he leaned forward and said, "I'm as horrified by what happened as you are. I had nothing to do with it."

The interviewer coughed. "Not many people believe that."

Tony smiled. "Lots of girls believe me. They write me letters, and I send them my poems."

I flinched.

When he asked if Tony had any more to say about the disappearance of Jessica Galvin, I held my breath. I couldn't shake the sense that he was staring straight at me as he said, "She's in California. It's the God's honest truth."

I turned it off.

Dicky tapped me on the shoulder.

"What?" I said.

"I saw him that night," he whispered.

I dropped my book. "Who?"

"Tony." His small fists were clenched tight as flower buds. "I went to the window when Jess woke me up with her scream. She was running and he was chasing her." He tilted his face to the side. "I thought it was a dream."

I exhaled slowly, remembering that voice I'd heard in the night. I'd thought it was a dream, too.

I went outside to wait for May and Sheila. May wanted to drive around in the sports car her dad had given her for birthday. Ever since I'd practically become famous for testifying against Tony, we'd started hanging out again. They said they were proud of me. I never asked about what they hadn't told me. We weren't close friends, but being around them was better than being alone.

Billy came walking out of his house. He and May weren't together anymore. Her new boyfriend looked like a blond Adonis and sold pot. As Billy was getting into his car, he smiled at me before driving away. We were going to the movies later. We'd gone on a few dates recently. His hair was longer now, and he wore it in a ponytail. He looked different, with an earring in one ear, and he didn't play football anymore. We still didn't agree on everything, but sometimes when I was with him I felt like I could begin again.

A few minutes later May showed up. I told her I loved her car and settled myself in the back seat.

She smiled. "Since the divorce, Ron has become a lot more generous."

"It must almost make the whole marriage breakup thing worth it," Sheila said and we all laughed a little too hard. Betty had found out that Ron was fooling around with his secretary and that she was only one of many. Mom never said anything about this unless you considered staring longingly out the window at nothing a statement.

May gunned the engine, and we headed into the desert. The white lines in the road stretched for miles ahead. She turned the radio up high and drove fast, the hot wind blowing in our faces. The Beatles came on singing "Strawberry Fields Forever." May and Sheila sang along, but I couldn't bring myself to join in the carefree refrain about nothing being real. A place where nothing is real wasn't my idea of a good time. Too many things that I'd thought were real had turned out not to be.

After we'd driven for a while, May pulled over. I looked at her questioningly. She took a camera out of the glove compartment. "Another birthday present from Ron. Come on, let's take a few pictures."

I dragged myself out of the car. It was blistering hot. The last thing I wanted was to walk around in the desert. I stood apart from them while she and Sheila clowned around with the camera. I'd grown suspicious of photos and the illusion they created that the past wasn't really gone. It was just another lie. Push aside the curtain and all that was left was something you didn't want to see.

May cocked her head. "What's wrong?"

"Nothing." I looked away. The sand was neither yellow nor white nor sprinkled with magic pink flowers, as I might have described it when I was younger. It was brown with purple shadows, gravel, and here and there a bleached-out cactus that reminded me of old fish bones. The desert went on and on, no one part of it distinguishable from another. In the distance, I saw something jutting up out of the sand. My body tensed as I walked toward it. All I could think of was a sneaker, dirty and untied, a sneaker that belonged to my sister. When I reached it though, it turned out to be just a rock.

I heard May and Sheila calling me, but I didn't turn. As I held the rock in my hand, I thought again of that voice in the night. Was the one thing that I'd dismissed as a dream the only thing that had actually been real? I pictured Jess, squinting at me, still wanting me to find her. Her fingers must have trembled as she stuffed the white shoe in her purse. She must have wanted to start a new life, but there was something she had to do first. She had to show the shoe to Tony that night. She had to confront him with what he'd done. When she said, "Would you," she was probably going to say something about the shoe, but I'd never know for sure. She must have told Tony she'd left the other one with me and that if he harmed her, his secret would be revealed. I imagined her screaming in his car as he drove her home, just as Billy had described it. And when he dropped her off out front to get the shoe, she must have changed her mind, and told him she was going to call the police. He blocked her way. And then she ran from him screaming, down the street and into the desert, her feet slipping in the sand, stumbling on the stones.

I dropped the rock and turned around. The brown scrub stretched as if to the edges of the earth. The sun was low in the sky. The cactus plants were rimmed with light. Everything was as it appeared to be.

"Caroline," May called out, "smile." I did, and she snapped my picture.

31901056767348